STAR WARS®
GALAXY of FEAR

THE SWARM

Bugs for breakfast?

The morning mist was already lifting and the sun had started to warm the ground. To his surprise, Zak found Tash and Hoole already up and sitting on the grass outside the ship. Bowls and containers were laid out in front of them.

"There you are!" Tash called. "Since the ship's power isn't working, and it's such a nice day, we thought we'd have a picnic of leftovers."

Zak plopped himself down beside his sister and picked up a bowl. It was full of leftover Circarpian snake eggs. They were cold, but scrambled just the way he liked them, and Zak dug in.

As he put the eggs in his mouth, he felt something wriggle against his lips.

Dropping his spoon, he looked into his bowl. A drog beetle was digging its way out of his breakfast.

Look for a preview of Star Wars: Galaxy of Fear #9, *Spore,* in the back of this book!

STAR WARS

GALAXY of FEAR

BOOK 8

THE SWARM

JOHN WHITMAN

BANTAM BOOKS
NEW YORK · TORONTO · LONDON · SYDNEY · AUCKLAND

To Judy McGuinn, for all she's done.

RL 6.0, 008–012

THE SWARM

A Bantam Skylark Book / February 1998

ISBN 0-553-48638-1

Published simultaneously in the United States and Canada

Bantam Books are published by Bantam Books, a division of Bantam Doubleday Dell Publishing Group, Inc. Its trademark, consisting of the words "Bantam Books" and the portrayal of a rooster, is Registered in U.S. Patent and Trademark Office and in other countries. Marca Registrada. Bantam Books, 1540 Broadway, New York, New York 10036.

PRINTED IN THE UNITED STATES OF AMERICA
OPM 0 9 8 7 6 5 4 3 2 1

PROLOGUE

Fresh air blew through the open windows, filling the small workshop with the beautiful scent of flowers.

The single figure in the workshop ignored the scent. He had more important things to do.

He sat down before a large, clear case. Within it, two tiny creatures frantically tried to crawl up the smooth sides. Wings fluttered on their backs, but they had nowhere to fly. They were his prisoners, but he had no intention of hurting them. He thought of himself as their caretaker.

Don't be afraid, the caretaker said to the two beetlelike creatures in a language only they could understand.

Immediately, the two crawlers stopped moving. On their heads, small antennae waved back and forth.

I am here to help you, the caretaker said.

The crawlers fluttered their wings and moved sharp-looking pincers back and forth.

The caretaker opened the glass case and reached inside. The two creatures jumped onto his arm and quickly scurried up to his shoulder.

I am your friend, the caretaker said. *I'll do whatever you need me to do.*

The creatures fluttered their wings again.

Outside the workshop, more wings fluttered in answer.

Thousands upon thousands of wings.

A dark cloud of wings fell over the little workshop, covering it in a blanket of crawling creatures.

Inside, the caretaker laughed.

CHAPTER 1

The hum of starship engines was music to Zak Arranda's ears.

He sat in the rear compartment of the *Shroud,* the ship in which he traveled with his sister, Tash, and his uncle Hoole. He was as close to the engines as he could be—probably closer than it was *safe* to be while they were operating. A thick layer of heat-resistant shielding separated him from the actual ion engines. Even so, the heat leaking through the durasteel walls was already making him and his clothes sticky with sweat. But Zak didn't care.

"So the hyperdrive motivator must connect to the main thrusters here," he said to himself, looking up from his small datapad and poking a finger at a thick piece of cable.

After a lot of searching through the ship's computer, Zak had finally found a diagram of the *Shroud*'s engines. The

3

diagram should have shown him everything he needed to know, but unfortunately, the *Shroud*'s previous owner had made a lot of changes. And the changes were what interested Zak. To a twelve-year-old boy who loved to take things apart and put them back together again, the starship was a flying playground.

One particular wire—a thick green-and-white-striped cable—caught Zak's eye.

"You know," said Zak to no one in particular, "I'll bet if I just connected this wire to the back-up power system, I could—"

Suddenly, the door behind him slid open. His sister stood in the doorway, her hands on her hips. "There you are," Tash Arranda said. "You know, we have a lesson with Uncle Hoole."

"Oh, yeah," Zak sighed. Hoole was a stickler for education. Even though Zak and Tash traveled constantly with their uncle and had not attended a regular school in months, they probably did more homework than any other twelve- and thirteen-year-olds in the galaxy. "When does it start?" he asked.

"Five minutes ago," Tash replied. "You're late."

"Be right there," Zak said.

Tash leaned over his shoulder and looked at the tangle of wires running through the wall to the powerful engines beyond. "Are you sure you should be messing around with that?"

4

"No problem," Zak said confidently. "Go on ahead. I'll be right there."

Tash gave her younger brother a doubtful look, then sighed and turned away. "Just be careful."

Zak grunted and waited until he heard the door slide shut. It wasn't that he didn't *like* Tash. He did. She was his sister and his best friend. They'd been through more together than most brothers and sisters. Their parents had died several months before when the Empire destroyed their homeworld, Alderaan. Luckily, Tash and Zak had been offworld at the time. And now they lived with their anthropologist uncle, Hoole—which meant they traveled all over the galaxy with him.

Even though Zak and Tash were brother and sister, they were very different from each other. Tash wasn't as interested in machines as Zak was. She liked to read and study. She was always using brainpower—especially since she'd become interested in the old Jedi Knights. Zak preferred anything that he could take apart and put back together with his own two hands.

"I'm sure I can boost the ship's power if I just disconnect this wire . . . ," he said. He plucked the wire from the wall. Nothing happened.

" . . . And connect it over here." He moved the thick wire to another panel in the wall, and looked for the right outlet. "There," he said, and stuck the wire into the wall.

Zzzzzzaaaaappp!

Electric current ran up Zak's arm, through his neck, and right into his head. Lightning flashed behind his eyeballs. A loud *pop!* followed, and Zak jumped backward as though a bantha had kicked him. Sparks flew from the panel.

The electrical tingle in Zak's body lasted only a few seconds. He checked his hands. They were hot, but he wasn't burned.

He had a feeling he was lucky.

Another loud *pop!* exploded from the panel in a shower of sparks. Zak froze. What had he done to the engines? What had he done to the ship? He waited a moment, but the engines continued to hum with their usual strength.

He had a feeling he was *really* lucky.

Zak hurried out of the engine room and down the corridor. A thin trail of smoke and the smell of burning metal followed him. What had caused that pop? What had he done wrong? And, more important . . . Should he tell Uncle Hoole?

Probably, was Zak's first thought.

But his second thought was, *Why bother?*

After all, the engines were still running perfectly. Whatever he'd done couldn't be that bad. It might not be worth mentioning. Besides, if he told Uncle Hoole, Tash would be sure to find out, and the last thing Zak wanted to hear was "I told you so" from her.

He decided to keep the accident a secret. The next time they landed, he'd give the engines a closer look and repair whatever little problem he might have caused. As long as the mistake was fixed, he told himself, no one else needed to know.

"Zak, you're late," Uncle Hoole said as Zak entered the *Shroud*'s small lounge area. His uncle cast a glance at Zak, his long, gray Shi'ido face looking stern as usual.

"Sorry, Uncle Hoole," Zak replied. "I didn't mean to miss the beginning of the lesson."

Hoole gave a small nod. "I'm afraid you've missed something else important. I just finished telling Tash about our destination."

"Destination?" Zak asked. "Have you found a safe place for us to hide from the Empire?"

Several months ago, Tash, Zak, and Hoole had become entangled in an Imperial plot. In the end, they had helped the Rebels foil the schemes of an Imperial scientist, but unfortunately they had also attracted the attention of the Emperor's most powerful servant—Darth Vader. Now they were on the run, traveling through the most remote parts of the galaxy, trying to avoid any Imperial contact while Hoole searched for a safe place to live.

"I'm afraid I haven't located a good hiding place as yet," the Shi'ido admitted. "But in the meantime, I've received word that the Empire is planning to establish a military outpost on the planet S'krrr."

Zak had never heard of S'krrr, but that didn't surprise him. There were thousands of civilized planets in the Empire. "So?" he asked. "The Empire has outposts everywhere."

"Not on S'krrr," Tash said. "At least not yet."

"Indeed," Hoole agreed. "And the real tragedy is that if the Imperials take over this planet, they will certainly destroy one of the most beautiful places in the entire galaxy— the Sikadian Garden. This garden is the cultural landmark of the people of S'krrr." Hoole paused. "I am determined to make sure the Empire doesn't destroy any more cultures."

Zak nodded. He knew his uncle's sad story all too well. Years ago, Hoole had been a scientist working for the Empire. The Empire had allowed one of Hoole's experiments to turn bad, and the resulting accident wiped out an entire race of beings. From that day on, Hoole had sworn he would protect as many civilizations as he could from Imperial cruelty.

A soft alarm sounded on the lounge's wall panel. "We're dropping out of hyperspace," Hoole said. "We must be near the planet now."

They hurried to the *Shroud*'s cockpit just in time to see the planet come into view. S'krrr was a beautiful blue-green world, with rolling clouds covering continents and oceans.

Zak felt his heart beat nervously as Hoole guided the ship down to the planet's surface. What if his little accident had damaged the landing gear? But the ship continued to glide smoothly through the air as Hoole spoke to S'krrr's planetary landing control.

The speaker on the other end of the link seemed to be

expecting Hoole. "The area near the Sikadian Garden is usually restricted," the voice said, "but you have permission to land just outside the garden walls."

Tash and Zak were impressed. "Do not be," Hoole advised. "It is simply that my reputation as an anthropologist gets me into some restricted spaces."

In minutes, the *Shroud* was zooming over the surface of the planet. On the horizon, they could see a wide, multicolored patch of ground that extended for several kilometers. Even at a distance, the Sikadian Garden looked beautiful.

The *Shroud* touched down outside a high wall covered in green vines. Even before they had come to a stop, a sweet, powerful smell filled the cabin.

"What's that?" Tash asked.

"Flowers from the garden," Hoole replied. "The scent is quite pleasant."

"And strong," she added, "if we can smell it right through the ship!"

"It probably came in through the air vents," Zak guessed. "I opened them up as we landed." Zak had opened them to help the engines cool—and to let the fresh air blow away the scent of burning wires. But he had decided not to tell Tash and Uncle Hoole about that.

As the ship finally settled on its landing gear, Zak let out a soft sigh of relief. Whatever he had done had obviously not hurt the ship.

"Zak, please go lower the ramp," Hoole requested.

"You bet!" Zak replied. He was so relieved he almost skipped down the corridor. At the exit hatch, he punched in the code that lowered the ramp and waited as the door slid open.

He stepped out into a bright, sunny day and smelled the scent of hundreds of growing flowers drifting toward him. He took a deep breath.

And then almost choked on it.

A giant insect, taller than Zak, came scuttling up the ramp. Its claws reached out to grab him.

CHAPTER 2

"Look out!" he yelled, stumbling back inside the ship and running into Hoole and Tash. "There's a giant bug out there! Close the door!"

It was too late. The creature had reached the doorway. It rubbed its two forelegs together, then jabbed one of the sharp, bladelike arms forward. Zak shrank back. "Uncle Hoole, help!"

Instead, Hoole reached out his own hand and touched the tip of the giant insect's leg.

"Welcome to S'krrr," the insect said in a soft, careful voice. "I am called Vroon."

Hoole bowed his head slightly. "I am Hoole. This is my niece, Tash. And this one," he added with a disapproving frown, "is called Zak."

"Welcome," the insect repeated.

The insect—Zak soon learned that they were called S'krrr, just like their planet—was shorter than Hoole and a little taller than Zak and Tash. The S'krrr walked—scuttled—on two legs, but its movements were very quick. Instead of hands, Vroon's arms ended in two bladelike tips that seemed to bend, so that he could pick up objects. His entire body was covered by a hard shell. Zak tried hard to think of the word for it. He was sure he had heard it during a biology lesson. Exoskeleton. That was it. A skeleton on the outside of the body. The S'krrr's entire body was hard and green except his belly, which was a soft, pale yellow.

Vroon's head was shaped like a triangle. Two enormous black eyes stared out from it. Vroon's mouth opened sideways, instead of up and down like a human's. Because of that, Zak couldn't tell if the S'krrr was amused or angry. His insectlike face was impossible to read.

Tash laughed. "Zak, I guess that'll teach you to miss a lesson."

"Right," was all he could say. "Sorry."

"No offense was taken," said the S'krrr in his soft voice. Something fluttered on his back, and for the first time, Zak noticed that the S'krrr had wings. They were small, pale, and transparent. It was obvious they would not allow Vroon to fly. But when he fluttered them together, the wings made a sound that was even softer than his voice. Zak heard a gentle *skrrrrr* fill the air for just a moment.

Then Vroon said, "However, you will have to move your ship."

Hoole raised an eyebrow. "We received permission from the planetary landing control—"

"The planetary landing control," Vroon said, his wings fluttering again, "controls planetary landing. It has no authority over the Sikadian Gardens. I do. I am the caretaker here, and I'm afraid that your ship is too close. The garden is a most delicate habitat, and the ship's noise and machinery might upset that balance. Please move it."

Hoole agreed. Zak could tell that his uncle didn't want to anger the garden's caretaker. Hoole entered the cockpit and tried to activate the *Shroud*'s repulsor lift engines.

Nothing happened.

Zak felt his stomach drop out.

"Strange," they heard Hoole mutter from the controls. Again they heard him throw the switch to activate the ship's engines, and again, nothing happened.

Hoole stepped out of the cockpit. "These engines were working at top performance only a few moments ago. I can't imagine what the problem might be."

Zak swallowed. Now he had to say something. "Um . . . I think I know what the problem might be."

"Yes, Zak?" Hoole asked.

"I think it might be me," he admitted. "I was—I was doing some work on the engines while we were in flight."

"I see." That was all Hoole said, but the Shi'ido had a habit of making a few words mean a lot. Zak almost wished he would shout, or at least get frustrated. Hoole's calm but disappointed face made Zak feel worse than any scolding.

13

Quickly, Zak told about the flying sparks and the loud popping sound. Hoole's look of concern deepened with every word. "Anyway," Zak said, "the engines were working fine afterward, so I figured nothing was wrong. I thought I could just fix it when we landed, and I wouldn't have to bother you with the problem."

Hoole shook his head. "That was a mistake. The ship's computer probably compensated for the problem during flight. But once we shut the ship down, the computers shut off."

Zak led the others to the engine room and showed Hoole what he had done. After a moment's study, Hoole shook his head. "I'm afraid this will take some time to correct."

Vroon's wings fluttered apprehensively. "Are you saying you cannot move your ship? That is unacceptable."

"I apologize," Hoole replied. "I would move the ship if I could, but that is impossible until it is repaired."

Again, the useless wings flapped quickly, which obviously meant Vroon was angry. "Clumsy offworlders," he muttered. "I expect you to do your best to remove this machine as soon as possible."

With that, the S'krrr turned and stalked away.

"I had better follow and make sure he does not take away our visiting privileges altogether," Hoole said. He hurried after their host, pausing only long enough to cast a warning glance at Zak. "Please make sure this is a lesson you *don't* miss."

"Wait!" Tash called out as Hoole walked away. "What are we supposed to do?"

"Look through the garden," their uncle suggested. "But be careful. Don't touch anything!"

Since the ship's power was out, none of the computers, games, or equipment worked. There was nothing to do but follow Hoole's suggestion.

Zak and Tash left the ship and walked toward the green wall that surrounded the garden. As they got nearer, they could see that the wall was actually a tall, thick hedge. Set into the hedge was an arched opening. The hedge wall looked very old, and Zak and Tash sensed that the S'krrr had been tending this garden for hundreds, maybe even thousands of years.

Passing under the arch, they entered the Sikadian Garden. Tash gasped. Even Zak, who was more interested in mechanical things than plants, whispered, "Prime."

The Sikadian Garden was the most beautiful place either of them had ever seen. A rock-lined path stretched out before them, winding through a grassy field and into a distant grove of trees. In various areas, thick patches of flowers of different shapes and sizes sprang up. Some were wide and flat like tabletops, others rose long and narrow, like the blade of a vibropike. They could hear the trickle of a waterfall in the distance.

The garden seemed completely natural. Tash and Zak walked for nearly a kilometer before they spotted anything artificially made. It was a small stone statue, sitting on the ground next to a small pond. It was covered with moss, and so crudely shaped that Zak thought it was just a rock. But on closer inspection, he saw that it was a carved stone statue of a bug. It looked somewhat like the S'krrr, but it walked on six legs instead of two.

"It looks old," Tash noted admiringly. "It's pretty good, too."

"Yeah," Zak said. "Someone really liked bugs, I guess. I wonder how they'd feel if they knew their art had ended up as a mound of moss." He turned and looked across the garden. "Now what?"

"Let's check out the flowers," Tash suggested.

"I'd rather look at rocks," her brother groaned. "Actually, I want to find that waterfall. I'll meet you back here."

The sound of trickling water seemed to come from beyond a grove of huge trees. Zak jogged down the path until he reached the shade of the trees. They had trunks as wide as a bantha's body. The leaves grew so thick and the branches rose up so high that beneath the tree it was as dark as nighttime.

But what caught Zak's eye was a strange mushroom that seemed to grow among the roots of the tree. The mushroom was gray, with a cap bigger than Zak's head. Dark spots covered the gray mushroom and Zak realized what had attracted his attention.

One of the spots was moving.

Creeping closer, Zak saw that the spot was a big beetle,

about as long as his finger. Two large, pale wings were folded over its back. Six double-jointed legs wiggled beneath its body as the insect scrambled across the mushroom cap. Two sharp pincers snapped open and shut as it crawled, as though it planned to eat the air. Three short, sharp antennae—almost like horns—jutted from its head. Now and then, the bug stopped to take a bite out of the mushroom with its snapping jaws.

Fascinated by the creature, Zak cautiously reached out to touch it. To his surprise, the bug crawled right onto his hand and continued walking.

"Hey, you're a nice little fellow, aren't you?" Zak said.

As he spoke, something big dropped from the trees above his head. With an ear-piercing shriek, the dark shape slammed into Zak's face.

CHAPTER

Zak didn't know what was worse, the shrieks coming from the creature's mouth, or the feel of its thick, leathery wings slapping against his face. He felt something sharp scratch his cheek and he threw his hands up to protect himself.

The flying creature swerved away, flapping furiously to gain some height. For an instant Zak got a good look at the creature. Its body was about one meter long, and it had even longer black wings. Its neck ended in a tiny head. A thin tail snaked through the air behind it.

The thing flapped up into the darkness of the tree.

But a moment later it plunged down again.

Zak threw himself to the ground as the beast swooped over him again. He grunted as the diving creature struck his back, then flapped away again.

"Help!" Zak yelled, but he could barely hear himself over the creature's weird shrieking noises.

Panicking, Zak felt around for something he could use as a shield or a weapon. His fingers wrapped around something dry and hard. A stick. A second later Zak nearly dropped the stick as he felt something sticky crawling along the back of his hand. He tried to shake it off, but it held on tight. It was the beetle.

The flying creature screeched and dove again. Desperately, Zak swung his stick around, hoping it would scare the creature away. His eyes were closed, but he felt the creature slam hard into his stick, snapping it in two. The shrieking stopped instantly. Then something fell to the ground with a thud.

Zak opened his eyes. He looked up. The creature was not there. He got to his knees and looked around, scanning the area until his eyes came to rest on a dark lump quivering on the ground.

"I don't believe it," he muttered as he tried to catch his breath. "What a lucky shot!"

But he knew it wasn't luck. The creature had swooped right into him, almost like it wanted to attack the stick, or his hand.

Zak got to his feet and stood over the creature. At first he'd thought it was some kind of bird, but now that it was still, he could see that it had no feathers. Instead, its body was covered with a layer of soft bluish hair except for its tail, which was thick and smooth like a dianoga's tentacle. Its head was long and narrow, and two rows of tiny, razor-sharp teeth stuck out from its mouth. The creature's wings were outspread, and its chest rose and fell rapidly as it panted for breath.

A second later, the panting stopped. Zak leaned closer—the creature wasn't breathing. It was dead.

"Oh, no," Zak groaned. The first thought that passed through his mind was, *Uncle Hoole is really going to be mad at me!* Hoole had warned them not to touch anything in the garden.

But his second thought was for the motionless creature. He hadn't meant to kill it. He was only trying to scare it away. But he wasn't going to waste time mourning. The creature *had* attacked him, after all.

Zak felt something tickle his fingers, and he glanced down in time to see the beetle hop off his hand and dart into the tall grass beneath the trees. "I don't blame you," Zak said, imagining Uncle Hoole's stern expression. "Maybe I should look for a place to hide, too."

Something stirred in the branches. Zak looked nervously up into the trees, wondering if there were more flying shriekers. Deciding that he didn't want to stick around and find out, Zak turned and hurried back the way he had come.

He found Tash just where he'd left her, admiring a patch of multicolored flowers. But Tash had been joined by a S'krrr. From the distance, Zak thought it was Vroon, but as he drew nearer he saw that this S'krrr was a few centimeters taller than the caretaker, and his hard shell was a darker shade of green. Still, this S'krrr's face looked exactly like Vroon's, and Zak wondered if all the S'krrr looked alike.

"Zak," Tash said, "this is Sh'shak."

"Greetings," said the S'krrr in an elegant voice, accompanied by the soft *skrrrr* sound as his small wings fluttered. "I am pleased to make your acquaintance."

"Hello," Zak answered as naturally as he could manage. He found it slightly uncomfortable talking to the S'krrr. Their hard-shelled faces were impossible to read. Zak could see his reflection in Sh'shak's large black eyes.

"Sh'shak is a celebrity here on S'krrr," Tash said. "He's a famous poet."

"Really? That's prime," Zak said without meaning it. He hated poetry.

Tash, however, loved reading, so it didn't surprise Zak when she asked the S'krrr, "Could you recite one of your poems?"

Sh'shak's dark eyes stared blankly at her. "I'm afraid you would not understand," he replied. "The poems are all in wingsong."

"Wingsong? What's that?" Zak asked.

In answer, Sh'shak fluttered his wings. As he listened, Zak heard the soft *skrrrrrrr* sound change its tone and pacing. By moving his wings at differing speeds, now rubbing them together, now fluttering them apart, Sh'shak created a series of intricate tones and humming noises. Even Zak had to admit that it was beautiful.

"That is wingsong," Sh'shak explained. "It is the traditional language of my people, a language we use to speak to each other. Of course, offworlders don't understand it and can't imitate the sounds, so we of S'krrr have learned the Basic language of the galaxy. But we still use wingsong, especially in writing poetry."

"Are you visiting the garden to look for new poem ideas?" Zak asked.

"In a sense," the S'krrr replied. "I come here to calm my mind and achieve balance. The garden is good for that. Balance is very important here."

Zak didn't understand. "Why?"

Sh'shak waved his sticklike forearm across the beautiful scene, taking in groves of trees, watery ponds, half a dozen patches of well-groomed flowers, and a sloping field of grass.

"This garden displays a delicate balance of nature," the S'krrr explained. "No modern technology is used here."

Boring, thought Zak. *I'd rather study power plants than living plants.*

Sh'shak continued. "No chemicals to make the flowers grow better, no insecticides are used to kill weeds or pests. Everything is done naturally."

"Wow," Tash said. "I remember our mom and dad once tried to grow a garden in our backyard at home. We had more weeds than vegetables!"

"And the bugs were the worst," Zak recalled. "They were everywhere!"

22

Sh'shak nodded. "Here in the Sikadian Garden, we encourage some insects to thrive. A certain type of beetle called a drog pollinates the flowers—"

"Pollinate?" Zak asked.

"Yes, they travel from plant to plant, spreading the pollen of one to the another. This helps the plants grow. But the insects themselves reproduce very quickly. They would soon overrun the entire garden, if they weren't kept under control."

"But you don't use pesticides?" Tash asked.

"We don't," Sh'shak replied. "The drog beetles have a natural enemy—the shreevs. Shreevs hunt the beetles, keeping the population under control. And this is where the true beauty of the garden takes place. The balance between the shreevs and the drogs is extremely delicate. In fact, legend has it that if even one shreev is killed before its natural time, the garden's balance will be destroyed."

"Really?" Tash asked, impressed. "Is that true?"

Sh'shak tilted his triangular head. "It is an old story, but who knows?"

"What do these shreevs look like?" Zak asked.

"Why, they look just like that," Sh'shak replied.

He pointed to a nearby tree. Clinging to a high branch sat a small, dark creature.

Just like the one Zak had killed.

CHAPTER

Zak's mouth went dry. He felt something heavy settle into the pit of his stomach.

"Th-That's a shreev?" Zak stammered. "And they're not supposed to be killed?"

"Not for any reason," Sh'shak replied.

"But what if one attacked us or something?" Zak asked. The feeling of dread in his stomach was growing. "Would it be all right then?"

Sh'shak considered. "It seems unlikely. Shreevs would never attack anything as large as a S'krrr or a human. They only hunt drogs. Besides, a shreev couldn't do any real damage to creatures our size. It would be wisest just to find cover or run away. The shreevs are protected by law."

Tash asked another question, but Zak didn't hear her. He was too busy listening to his pounding heart.

He had killed a shreev.

He'd broken the law.

But no one knew about it.

The thought crept into his brain like a whispered secret. No one knew. Besides, it was an accident. He had only meant to scare the shreev away, but the creature had flown right at him. It wasn't his fault.

"Zak, is something wrong?" Tash asked him, looking at him strangely.

Zak shrugged. "Well, yeah. A little while ago, I was—"

"Zak, Tash, there you are," Uncle Hoole said. He was hurrying down the path with Vroon at his side. Despite the difference in their heights, the S'krrr moved quickly on its sharply-jointed legs. The caretaker had no trouble keeping pace with Hoole's gliding steps.

"I have excellent news," Hoole said. "Vroon has seen fit to allow the ship to remain where it is until it is fixed and we are ready to depart."

"As long as it isn't activated," Vroon said. "I don't want your energy fields harming my garden."

"Certainly not," Hoole agreed dryly. He looked at Sh'shak. "I see you two have made an acquaintance of your own."

Tash introduced them. "This is Sh'shak. Sh'shak, this is our uncle Hoole."

"Uncle?" the S'krrr looked at Tash questioningly. "You are human, are you not? And you, sir, are—"

"A Shi'ido," Hoole confirmed.

"Uncle Hoole adopted us," Zak explained. "Our parents died about eight months ago—"

"Nine months now," Tash put in.

"—nine months," Zak agreed. Sadly, he realized how quickly the time had passed since it had happened. "They were on Alderaan when the Empire destroyed the planet."

Sh'shak paused a moment, then bowed his head. His wings fluttered a low, sad note. But in Basic, his voice was hard. "These are sad times," the S'krrr said.

Zak thought he heard anger in Sh'shak's voice and looked at Tash. The Arrandas knew that they weren't the only people in the galaxy who'd been hurt by the Empire. Zak wondered if Sh'shak might be a Rebel sympathizer.

"Are you *the* Sh'shak?" Hoole asked. "I have heard your name mentioned several times since I began studying your planet. You are quite famous here."

Sh'shak ran his arm across the top of his hard shell head. "I am known among my people," he said modestly.

"Poetry must be *really* popular here," Zak said, raising his eyebrows.

Vroon spoke up. "Oh, it's not his poetry that's made him so famous here. He has a far more . . . aggressive talent."

Sh'shak's forearms twitched. "As I said, I have the honor of being known among my people. But perhaps there are more interesting things to talk about than a humble S'krrr such as me. Have you seen the garden yet, Hoole?"

Zak could tell Sh'shak wanted to change the subject, but

26

now he was interested in what Vroon had said. What did he mean by an "aggressive talent"?

But he had no time to ask as Vroon eagerly led them back down the garden path and toward a small cottage.

The cottage was very old-fashioned. There wasn't a bit of durasteel or plastic anywhere on the outside—just moss-covered stones and a slanted wood roof. Vroon explained why. "All natural materials are used to ensure that no technology interferes with the true course of nature."

Even the inside of the cottage was old-fashioned. The doors didn't automatically slide open and shut—they had to be opened and shut by hand. Wooden tables lined the walls, and on these tables lay trays of seeds, and pots filled with small, growing flowers.

"There's no glass or transparasteel on the windows," Zak noticed. "Everything is wide open."

"Of course, of course," Vroon hummed. "The shreevs would not be able to see the glass." Vroon made a quick, high-pitched fluttering sound with his wings that sounded almost like a chuckle. "The stupid creatures would fly right into them. And of course we can't have that."

The visitors continued touring the cottage, as Vroon showed them his various projects. One particular plant had caught Tash's attention. Next to it sat the only real piece of scientific equipment in the workshop. Several wires had been attached to the broad green leaves of the plant. The wires led to a small recording device with a digital display screen.

As she examined it, and Hoole and Sh'shak entered into a discussion of their own, Zak decided to get some information from Vroon. "Is that legend true?" Zak asked as matter-of-factly as possible. "If one shreev is killed before its time, the whole balance of nature in the garden is thrown off?"

"Very true," Vroon said. A gleam appeared in his eye as he turned to study the young human. "The Sikadian Gardens are extremely delicate. The slightest change could mean complete and utter disaster."

Zak swallowed. "I can't believe this place is that . . . um" —he searched for a word—"breakable."

Vroon's wings fluttered irritably. "Oh, you can't, can you? Let me show you something."

Vroon led Zak to a table across the room. On the table, something lay covered by a large square of cloth. Vroon pulled back the cloth to reveal a glass container filled with the same large beetles—drog beetles—Zak had seen earlier. There were many of them, crawling and swarming over one another in the container. Their legs worked frantically as they tried to crawl up the sides of the glass. Every once in a while, one of the drogs would flutter its wings and leap up, only to slam against the top of the container.

Vroon leaned close to the container. "Aren't they beautiful?"

"Um, yeah, I guess," Zak agreed politely. *Beautiful* was not the word he would have chosen.

"How many do you count?" Vroon asked.

Zak paused. "Twelve. No, thirteen."

Vroon nodded. "Yesterday, there were two. Drog beetles reproduce very quickly. Fortunately, the average shreev eats thirty beetles a day. Then they generally sleep for the rest of the day, which is also fortunate. If they ate more than thirty, they might wipe out the drog beetles. As it is, they eat just enough to control the population."

"Shreevs eat the drog beetles," Zak asked, "but what do the beetles eat?"

"Everything," Vroon replied. "They move from plant to plant, eating the nectar off the leaves and helping to spread pollen. But they're also scavengers. They'll eat fungus, and even dead animals if they get the chance. That's partly why they reproduce so quickly, because they can survive on anything. Imagine what would happen if every two drog beetles produced twelve new insects every day. We'd be overrun!"

Zak felt his heart sink. *I'd better tell them,* he decided. *Maybe there's something Vroon can—*

"Excuse me," Tash called out. "What's this?" She was standing over the wired plant.

Vroon went over to her. "That is a failed experiment. I was doing research into plant communication. I was hoping to find a way to talk with some of the flora we have here."

"Talking to *plants*?" Zak said disbelievingly.

Vroon's large eyes regarded him. "Of course. The plants don't actually *speak,* of course. But it's a known fact that plants react to different types of music. Some scientists even believe that plants can sense the difference between an angry, violent person and a calm, gentle person. This instrument" —he pointed at the digital readout— "measures the plant's chemical reactions."

"So you can, in a way, tell what it's thinking, or how it's feeling?" Tash asked.

"Exactly," Vroon replied. "But the experiment has proved imprecise. It's too difficult to measure the findings."

Tash turned to look for Hoole, who was still talking quietly with Sh'shak. "Hey, Uncle Hoole, you should see this!"

Meanwhile, Zak studied the small instrument attached to the wires. "Well, I think part of the problem is that this wire isn't attached. Here, try this."

He clipped the wire back into the instrument just as Hoole and Sh'shak reached the worktable. Instantly, the digital display came alive. A bright line shot across the small screen, bouncing up and down in frantic, jagged movements.

Tash looked at the plant. It was as still as any potted plant, but the sensor readout made it look like a jumble of nerves. "This plant is upset," she observed.

"Perhaps it isn't used to so many visitors," said Vroon. "I lead a rather reclusive and busy life. Which reminds me, I have much work to do. If you'll excuse me . . ."

It was clear that Vroon had had enough of them for one day. Uncle Hoole promised the caretaker that his research on S'krrr was for a good cause—he wanted to make sure the rest of the galaxy knew about the S'krrr culture before the Empire tried to destroy it. He also promised that his work would only last a day or two, and then they would be gone.

The rest of their afternoon was uneventful. Sh'shak agreed to see them again soon, and excused himself. Zak and Tash followed Hoole back to the *Shroud,* where they ate a cold dinner ("Thanks to Zak," Tash grumbled), and went to sleep.

For Zak, the evening and the night could not pass quickly enough. Because Vroon's comments had given him an idea.

The next morning he woke early and pulled on his flight suit. As quietly as he could, he slipped out of the *Shroud* and headed for the garden.

Thick morning mist had settled over the beautiful grounds, dampening all the bright colors of the day before. Zak didn't care. He hadn't come to look at flowers.

Following the same path he'd chosen before, he entered the grove of trees and started to look around. At first he couldn't see anything but morning mist, the trunks of trees, mushrooms, and flowers. But slowly, his eyes adjusted, and he detected movements on leaves and petals.

Drog beetles.

Once he got used to looking for them, it became easier to spot the insects crawling from place to place. Zak picked a flowering bush that was nearly covered in the bugs. He flicked several of the insects off their perches and onto the ground.

Then he crushed them underfoot.

"Sorry," Zak said. He supposed it didn't make any difference to the drog beetles whether the shreev ate them or he stomped on them. All that mattered was that nature was kept in balance.

Zak kept on stomping until he'd crushed exactly thirty—the number of drog beetles the shreev would have eaten if Zak hadn't killed it.

When he was done, he headed back toward the *Shroud*. For one day at least, Zak had been able keep his troubles at bay. He figured he could do the same tomorrow, and the next day, as long as they stayed on the planet. After that, he didn't know what he'd do.

"I'll think of something," he muttered to himself. "I hope."

The morning mist was already lifting and the sun had started to warm the ground. To his surprise, Zak found Tash and Hoole already up and sitting on the grass outside the ship. Bowls and containers were laid out in front of them.

"There you are!" Tash called. "Since the ship's power isn't working, and it's such a nice day, we thought we'd have a picnic of leftovers."

Zak plopped himself down beside his sister and picked up a bowl. It was full of leftover Circarpian snake eggs. They were cold, but scrambled just the way he liked them, and Zak dug in.

He felt better. As long as he did the work the shreev would have done, no one would know he'd broken any local laws. He scooped up another spoonful of eggs, telling himself that everything was going to work out just fine.

As he put the eggs in his mouth, he felt something wriggle against his lips.

Lowering his spoon, he looked into its bowl. A drog beetle was digging its way out of his breakfast.

CHAPTER

Zak grabbed a napkin and wiped the egg off his face.

"Yuck!" Tash said, scrambling out of the beetle's way. The insect scurried into the grass and vanished. "How'd *that* get into our food?"

"We are on the edge of the garden, remember," Hoole said calmly. "We are bound to encounter some of the more uncomfortable aspects of nature. It is nothing to worry about."

Zak shuddered. He could still feel the drog beetle's legs scratching against his lips. "Easy for you to say. You didn't almost *eat* one!"

Suddenly, Tash looked up. "Uh-oh, it looks like that's not the only pest in the garden."

A high-pitched whine grew louder as she spoke. In the distance, an Imperial shuttle glided toward them. It passed directly over their heads, then over the garden wall, and settled to a landing inside the garden.

"Vroon's not going to like that," said Zak.

"Neither do I, if the Empire's after *us*," Tash replied.

"Remain calm, Tash," Uncle Hoole advised. "If the Empire knew we were here and wanted to arrest us, they would have sent an armored gunboat and stormtroopers, not a shuttle. This could merely be a coincidence."

"But what if it's not?" she asked.

Hoole gave a slight shrug. "We would not have a chance to escape anyway, since our ship is not functional."

Zak felt a twinge in his chest. It was his fault the ship was grounded. And it was his fault the shreev had died. He almost wished he were a drog beetle, so he could crawl underneath the nearest rock and hide.

That feeling only grew stronger as three men appeared. They walked out of the garden through the arch, and marched directly toward the *Shroud*. Zak, Tash, and Hoole tensed. Even from a distance, Zak could see that all three men wore the uniforms of Imperial officers. Beside him, Uncle Hoole gave a slight shiver. A weird ripple drifted across his skin, and Zak knew that his uncle was preparing to use the Shi'ido power that had saved them so many times before—the power to shapechange into any creature in the galaxy.

The Imperials reached them moments later. Two of the officers were typical sharp-eyed, hard-nosed human Imperials. But the third, who seemed to be the leader, was very unusual. He looked human, except that his skin was pale blue, and his eyes were as red as blood.

"You there," the blue-skinned Imperial said. His speech reminded Zak of Hoole's—short, precise sentences spoken in a hard voice. But unlike Hoole, this Imperial's voice was cold. "I am Captain Thrawn, commander of the Imperial Star Destroyer *Vengeance*. I am looking for the caretaker of this garden. Where is he?"

Zak and Tash both sighed with relief, and even Uncle Hoole relaxed slightly. So this Captain Thrawn wasn't coming for them after all.

"The caretaker's name is Vroon," Uncle Hoole replied. "His workshop is half a kilometer to the west, alongside the garden wall."

Thrawn nodded. "Excellent. I must speak with him immediately."

"Why? So you can tell him he's out of a job?" Tash said. Zak was surprised at the forcefulness in her voice. He knew how much she disliked the Empire, but he couldn't believe she would be so outspoken before the captain of an Imperial Star Destroyer.

But she wasn't done. "Are you going to let Vroon know that the Empire is on its way to take over S'krrr?"

The two junior officers growled irritably. "Wolver, Tier, at ease," Thrawn ordered. The Imperial captain merely gazed at Tash with his bright red eyes. "If the Empire ever decided to take over S'krrr, no such warning would be given," he stated. "We would simply take it. But I assure you I am as much a visitor to the Sikadian Gardens as, I assume, you are. I have come to study S'krrr art—especially the garden."

"How curious, Captain," said Hoole. "I am an anthropologist, and I am here for much the same reason. I think you will find the garden a most informative means of studying the S'krrr culture."

A small, evil smile crept across Thrawn's lips. "That is what I hope."

Tash folded her arms across her chest and scowled. "I never realized Imperial captains were art lovers."

Thrawn looked mildly amused by Tash's defiant tone. "I find the information useful," he said. "The more insight I have into a culture, the more easily I can . . . *deal* with it."

The way Thrawn said the word *deal* made Zak's blood run cold.

Thrawn spun around and marched off without another word, his junior officers following. As soon as they were out of earshot, Tash asked, "Uncle Hoole, do you think he's telling the truth?"

Hoole shook his head. "I do not know, but I am sure he has not come to arrest us. He probably does not realize we are fugitives from the Empire."

"Thank the stars for that," Zak put in. "The last thing I want to see is the inside of an Imperial detention center."

"Indeed," Hoole replied. "But still, I am uneasy. Captain Thrawn is here for some reason, and I am sure it means trouble for anyone who gets in his way. We must be cautious.''

Hoole insisted that they spend the day near the ship. Zak was happy to oblige—it gave him a chance to help repair the *Shroud*. But Tash was disappointed. She had wanted to visit Sh'shak in the garden. Instead she was forced to watch Zak and Hoole tinker with the starship's engines for most of the day. By the time they quit that evening, she was bored out of her mind and restless.

Hoole was inside the *Shroud,* using the small emergency generator to cook their evening meal. The sun had half set, spreading a dark orange glow across the horizon. Tash and Zak lay on their backs on the ship's entry ramp, looking up at the darkening sky. Above them, dark shapes swooped and whirled in circles, sending high-pitched calls into the cooling air. The shreevs had come out to hunt.

''It's just not fair,'' Tash was saying. ''Uncle Hoole should have let me go see Sh'shak. How many chances am I going to get to spend a whole day with a real poet and philosopher?''

''One chance is one too many, if you ask me,'' Zak replied sarcastically. But his mind was elsewhere. The shreevs circling above his head reminded him that he still hadn't told anyone about his accident.

''Tash, I've got to tell you something—''

''Zak,'' Tash interrupted. ''I want to ask you a favor.''

He paused. ''Sure. Name it.''

She pushed a strand of blond hair behind her ear. ''I want

to go check out the Imperial shuttle tomorrow morning. Will you come with me?"

"What's there to see?" he asked.

"I don't know," his sister admitted. "I just think that Thrawn is up to something. It's just a *feeling*."

Zak knew all about Tash's feelings. She was in touch with the Force, the mysterious power that gave the ancient Jedi Knights their abilities. Over the last few months, Zak had learned to listen to Tash and her feelings.

"Okay," he said.

"Great. I'll wake you early," she said. "Oh, did you want to tell me something?"

"Your meal is prepared," Hoole's voice called from inside the ship.

Zak sighed. "It can wait."

That evening passed more quickly than the one before. Zak had convinced himself that as long as he kept killing beetles, he could prevent the garden from being damaged. That comforted him enough to help him sleep well, until he felt something tickling his ear well before sunrise. He tried to brush it away, but it kept tickling him. Finally, he opened his eyes to find Tash sitting beside his bed.

"Get up," she said.

Zak blinked. His eyes were too full of sleep to read his chrono. "You've got to be kidding," he groaned.

"You promised," Tash said.

Grunting, Zak dragged himself out of bed and into his clothes. He was still rubbing sleep out of his eyes as he followed Tash out of the *Shroud* and through the garden arch. The sky was turning from black to gray.

The Imperial shuttle was not far away. They could see its bulk through the morning mist, crouched like a giant predator waiting to strike.

Zak yawned. "Great, it's an Imperial shuttle. Can I go back to bed now?"

"No," Tash replied in a lowered voice. "I have a feeling something's going to happen."

"Sure," Zak said. "If we stand here long enough, we can watch the shuttle rust. Tash, even secret Imperial plots don't get going until after breakfast—"

He didn't finish his sentence. With a quiet *whirrr,* a small hatch opened beneath the shuttle. Zak felt Tash pull him down to the ground just as a shadowy figure slipped out of the shuttle, paused to make sure no one had seen him, then dashed off into the garden.

Even in the misty dawn light, Tash and Zak had both seen the blaster in his hand.

"I told you!" Tash whispered. "They're up to something!'

"Maybe," Zak whispered back. "But Imperials always carry blasters."

"Yeah, but they only draw them when they're going to shoot someone!" Tash started after the shadowy figure.

As loud as he dared, Zak called after her, "Even if there is something going on, what are we going to do about it?"

Tash didn't answer until Zak had caught up with her. "I

don't know," she said, "but Uncle Hoole said he was determined not to let the Empire destroy any more civilizations. Considering what happened to Alderaan, we should do our part, too. Maybe if we follow this Imperial, we'll find out what's going on, and we can tell Uncle Hoole. He'll know what to do."

The plan seemed harmless enough to Zak. After spending all day yesterday stuck near the *Shroud,* he was ready to be talked into a walk in the Sikadian Garden. And if they were caught, they could claim they had been doing just that—going for an early morning walk.

It was easy to move quietly on the damp grass, so they ran at nearly full speed in the direction the shadowy figure had gone. They caught sight of him once or twice—just a glimpse, but it was enough to keep on his trail.

But the figure didn't seem to have any set route. He was moving quickly, but aimlessly, dashing in and out of trees, zigzagging among rows of flowers, and circling around a large pond.

Tash and Zak followed his trail until it ended in some bushes. They crawled through the thick, prickly plants, and when they came out the other side, the shadowy figure was gone.

"Well," Zak panted, "so much for that plan."

"Oh, laserburn!" Tash said, kicking at the wet ground. "I hope we didn't miss our chance to spy on those Imperials."

A moment later a faint hum drifted toward them, like the

soft buzz of a power generator. Following the sound, the two Arrandas found themselves climbing a small hill covered in tiny glowing flowers. The hum came from the top of the rise. Silently, they crept upward.

Now they heard soft grunts and quick footsteps. The hum sounded like the *vrrooom* of a slashing vibroblade. Was there a fight going on above them?

Zak and Tash crawled on their hands and knees, staying low as they reached the crest of the hill. They gasped when they saw who was there.

CHAPTER 6

"Sh'shak!" Tash gasped in spite of herself.

Sh'shak froze instantly. He was alone, holding a wicked-looking staff with a blade at one end. He held the weapon over his head, poised to strike a small tree that was growing at the top of the hill. The sapling already had dozens of marks where Sh'shak's weapon had cut the bark. None of the slashes were deep enough to hurt the tree, but all of them were long and precise.

Zak and Tash found it hard to believe this was the same peaceful S'krrr they had met only yesterday. He looked violent and warlike. There was a fierce fire in his black eyes.

But Sh'shak's warlike manner vanished the instant he saw them. In a smooth, practiced motion he lowered his weapon and stuck the bladed end into the ground. His arms dropped calmly to his sides and his face took on the serene look they had seen when they first met him. In one second he had changed from a warrior back into a gentle poet.

Sh'shak took a few steps away from the tree. "Tash, Zak," he said gently. His wings fluttered on his back. "This is a pleasant surprise."

"It's a surprise, anyway," Zak muttered.

"Sh'shak, what are you doing?" Tash asked, pointing at the weapon sticking out of the ground.

"Ah, this," he said. "Just practicing."

"Practice!" Zak scoffed. "Since when do poets practice with vibropikes?"

Sh'shak's wings fluttered again. "I have many interests. Now, if you'll excuse me, I have work to do elsewhere." Quickly, the S'krrr pulled his weapon out of the ground and hurried off. He was gone in a moment.

"Well, Tash, is this what you expected to find?" Zak said. "It looks like your friend the poet doubles as a trained killer!"

Tash shook her head. "Remember the other day when Vroon said Sh'shak had a more aggressive talent? Maybe this is what he meant."

"Maybe," Zak replied, recalling the scene in the caretaker's hut yesterday. "And maybe that plant the other day went crazy because of Sh'shak. We've both met our share of weirdos in the past few months, and I'm starting to think your friend may belong on the list."

44

"Because he practices a little self defense?" Tash retorted.

"Self defense?" her brother replied, pointing to the tree trunk Sh'shak had scarred. "Tell that to the tree!"

By now the mist had cleared and the sun had risen high enough to light the entire garden. Tash and Zak hurried back to the *Shroud*, hoping Hoole might help them make some sense out of what they had seen.

But before they reached the ship, they met another figure strolling through the garden. Captain Thrawn stood at the edge of one of the many flower beds that dotted the landscape. In this bed, the flowers had been arranged in color patterns. Most of the flowers had white petals, but some with blue petals had been planted to form swirls in the white fields. Thrawn stood with his hands behind his back, studying the flowers as though they were the secret of the universe.

"Interesting," he muttered to himself as they passed by. "Most revealing."

"What do you know?" Zak whispered to Tash. "He really is a nut for flowers."

Thrawn overheard him. Without looking at Zak, the blue-skinned Imperial replied, "You are only a child, so I will forgive your insolent behavior. This time." He paused. "What you fail to realize is that a culture reveals itself through its art. If you know how to read the art, you will find everything you need to know about the people."

Tash frowned. "And that's information you can use against them."

"When necessary," Thrawn replied. He still hadn't bothered to look at them.

"I knew the Empire was up to something here," Tash said.

Finally Thrawn turned. His red eyes burned into Tash so fiercely that at first she blushed, then her face went pale with fear. But when he spoke, Thrawn's voice was calm. "I am waiting for a message from one of my officers, and I have little time, so I will be brief. I encounter civilians like you all the time. You believe the Empire is continually plotting to do harm. Let me tell you, your view of the Empire is far too dramatic. The Empire is a government. It keeps billions of beings fed and clothed. Day after day, year after year, on thousands of worlds, people live their lives under Imperial rule without seeing a stormtrooper or hearing a TIE fighter scream overhead."

Thrawn started to walk away, and motioned for Zak and Tash to follow him. They didn't dare disobey. "I assure you, I am part of no plot against the S'krrr. I find them a most interesting race. I came here to study them because they are quite different from most humanoid species. I assume you know that the S'krrr evolved from insects?"

Tash and Zak nodded. Given the S'krrr's appearance, it was easy enough to guess.

"Based on the art I've studied," the Imperial continued,

"and the way they use this garden as an expression of their culture, I'd say the S'krrr worship both beauty and violence. The garden is well-ordered, but it is also natural and wild. It shows the two sides of the S'krrr personality.

"But the most interesting thing about the S'krrr," Thrawn continued, talking more to himself than to the Arrandas, "is that for many years a cult existed in S'krrr society that *worshipped* insects. This cult believed that insects were the S'krrr's ancestors, and should be respected and revered. For a number of years, this worship became the center of their art. The S'krrr were forbidden to harm the insects, and the insects were encouraged to expand and grow."

Zak spoke up. "We found a statue of a bug the other day. It was old and worn, but you could still tell what it was."

Thrawn nodded. "This garden was originally the place where the insects were worshipped."

"But the S'krrr don't worship insects anymore," Tash observed.

"No," Thrawn agreed. "The cult was forbidden when the insects threatened to overrun the entire planet. But rumor has it that many S'krrr still follow the old beliefs."

He paused a moment. "You see, that is all the information I'm looking for here. I simply believe in knowing as much about a culture as possible. And I assure you, that I have no intention of wasting my time with any fiendish plots."

47

Tash started to respond, but the words caught in her throat and she gagged. Beside her, Zak felt his stomach leap into his throat as he saw what she was looking at.

Lying in the path before them was the body of an Imperial officer. They could barely make out his face, because almost every piece of exposed skin was swarming with beetles.

CHAPTER 7

Zak and Tash rushed forward to help the officer. Thrawn remained behind, studying the scene with cold efficiency.

Zak and Tash both fell to their knees, trying to brush the swarming drog beetles from the Imperial's body. Some of the beetles landed in the grass and waddled away to investigate other things, but most merely opened their wings and fluttered back toward the body.

"Help us!" Zak called out to Thrawn.

"Don't bother," the Imperial captain replied. "He's dead."

Thrawn was right. The body wasn't moving. The officer's skin was already pale and cold. Zak could see wriggling bulges in his uniform where the beetles had crawled under his clothes.

Something bit Zak. "Ow!" he yelled, leaping back.

Tash looked up. "Zak, what's— Ow!" She jumped to her feet, too, sticking her finger in her mouth. "One of those things bit me!"

"Me too," Zak said. He looked at his hand. There was a tiny red mark. "I guess they don't want us interfering with their meal." He shuddered.

Behind them, Captain Thrawn pulled a comlink from his belt and spoke to someone on the other end, probably on board the Star Destroyer orbiting overhead. "This is Captain Thrawn. Order the entire Sikadian Garden sealed. All ships within one thousand kilometers are to be grounded immediately, then searched. Someone has murdered Lieutenant Wolver."

Thrawn moved with lightning-fast efficiency. Tash and Zak watched as, for the next hour, Imperial investigators shuttled down from Thrawn's Star Destroyer to examine the area. A medical team examined the body where it lay. Imperial crewmen cut tree branches and uprooted bushes, using them as brushes to drive the swarming beetles away.

As they did, Vroon seemed to materialize out of nowhere. His wings hummed angrily, and he said, "I must protest! This garden is a protected area. You can't just come in here, tearing up the plants. And the beetles! You must not—"

Thrawn waved him off. "I will do whatever I must. One of my men has been murdered. The investigation is more important than your bugs."

But Vroon continued to complain until Thrawn ordered

his men to take the caretaker away. At that, Vroon hurried off, complaining as he disappeared down one of the garden's many paths.

Once the drog beetles were removed from the body, the medical examiner found several large wounds.

"What caused the wounds?" Thrawn demanded.

"Difficult to say," the doctor replied. "I'm not sure if they were made before the beetles did their work, or if the insects crawled into the existing holes and made them wider. But I would say that, if anything, the wounds were made by a very large handweapon, perhaps a vibropike."

Zak and Tash looked at each other, remembering Sh'shak.

Thrawn spoke through his comlink. "Thrawn to Star Destroyer *Vengeance*. Begin monitoring all planetary transmissions. It's possible that there is an anti-Imperial group operating on S'krrr. They may have murdered Lieutenant Wolver. Keep me informed."

Tash and Zak slipped off while Thrawn was giving orders for the body's removal, and returned to the *Shroud*.

They found Hoole waiting with a frown etched deeply into his face. The interior of the *Shroud* looked like it had been torn apart by Tusken Raiders.

"Zak, Tash, I'm relieved to see you here. Stormtroopers marched through here and searched the *Shroud*. They would not say what they were looking for."

"They were looking for a murderer!" Zak replied.

"We were with Captain Thrawn. We found one of his

51

officers. The man was dead, and there were drog beetles all over him." She shuddered.

Zak added, "And you won't believe it. Earlier, we saw—"

He stopped. Sh'shak had suddenly appeared.

"Oh," Zak ended lamely.

"Yes, Zak?" Hoole prodded.

Zak swallowed. "Nothing. It's just that Captain Thrawn thinks there are anti-Imperial agents on the planet."

Sh'shak's wings hummed. "Most interesting. If that is the case, the Imperials may declare a curfew. I must finish some errands before they do so." He bowed to Hoole. "It was a pleasure speaking with you. Good day."

Zak waited until the S'krrr was out of sight. "He's the murderer!"

Hoole blinked. "Nonsense."

"But we saw him practicing with a vibropike!" Zak insisted. "He looked like a killing machine."

"I think Zak may be right, Uncle Hoole," Tash admitted. "Sh'shak told me he was a poet, but after what I saw today . . ."

Hoole shook his head. "Zak, Tash, this is where an understanding of alien cultures can help you. You see, the S'krrr are—"

Hoole's sentence was cut off by the sound of pounding on the ship's hull. Hoole looked outside to find Thrawn's other lieutenant, Tiers, waiting. "You are to come with me," he said to Hoole.

"But I have not done anything," Hoole replied.

"Captain Thrawn is questioning everyone," Lieutenant Tiers declared. He pointed at Zak and Tash. "They can remain behind."

Hoole was gone a long time. Zak and Tash could do nothing but wait impatiently, pacing the corridors of the *Shroud,* tapping their fingers against the powerless computer monitors.

"Do you think Sh'shak did it?" Zak finally asked. "Do you think he's a Rebel?"

"Maybe, to the first question," his sister replied. "But I doubt it to the second. Think about the Rebels we've met in the past. Luke Skywalker and Princess Leia, and even Wedge a few months ago. They were willing to fight for what they believed in, but none of them were cold-blooded killers."

"And neither, it seems, am I," said Uncle Hoole, suddenly stepping through the door.

"Uncle Hoole!" the Arrandas shouted together. "You're all right!"

"Indeed," Hoole replied, "although it was touch and go for a while. I make rather a suspicious character these days, it seems. Previously, I could use my credentials as an anthropologist to explain my travels. But now it hardly seems wise to mention my true name, since we're all wanted by the Empire."

Hoole explained that he'd managed to convince the Imperials that he and the two Arrandas were on a cultural field trip. Since he could prove he'd been at the *Shroud* working on the engines all morning, the rest of his story worked.

Tash tried to break in. "Uncle Hoole, there's something we should tell you about Sh'shak . . ."

But Hoole was already heading toward his cabin. "I'm afraid it will have to wait until morning, Tash. I am quite weary from the questions, and I must consider how we can leave this planet safely, and soon."

As he entered his room, he added, "There will be more questions in the morning. Thrawn has sent most of his men back to his Star Destroyer, but he is determined to find the murderer. We should all get some rest to prepare ourselves for more questioning tomorrow."

Zak went to his cabin, shoved a pile of clothes, datacards, and his trusty skimboard off the bed, slipped into a sleep suit, and finally fell in a heap on the bunk. He'd gotten up early that morning, and he was tired. Their visit to S'krrr was turning into a nightmare. Now, even if they'd fixed the *Shroud*'s engines, Thrawn could keep them grounded until he found the killer.

Killer! Zak's heart skipped a beat. In all the excitement, he'd forgotten about the shreev he killed. He'd forgotten to kill thirty beetles! Frantically, he tried to remember if the Imperials had killed any while they examined the body. Were the beetles just driven off, or were they crushed? And if some were crushed, how many?

Zak groaned. "You blew it again, Zak Arranda."

But then he tried to calm down. Missing one day

couldn't be that bad, could it? After all, he could always try to get sixty of the beetles tomorrow.

He nodded. That would do it. He'd simply catch up tomorrow. With that comforting thought, Zak drifted off to sleep.

He woke up hours later in the dark. Something was tickling his ear. He yawned. "Tash, stop it. Go away."

Something tickled his ear again. "Tash, I don't care who you want to spy on now, I'm staying in bed." He opened his eyes.

Tash wasn't there.

Tiny legs scampered across his cheek and scurried up into his hair. Slapping at it, Zak sat up and snapped on his cabin lights.

His bed was covered with drog beetles.

CHAPTER

8

A beetle jumped onto his hand and started to scramble up his sleeve. Another one landed right on the end of his nose, its wings still outstretched.

"Help!" Zak screamed. He threw off his bedcovers, sending a shower of beetles scattering around his room. Zak could hear the hard shells of the beetles clacking against the floor, and he felt their scratching claws pluck at his skin. He slapped at his arms and chest beneath his shirt.

The door to Zak's room slid open. Tash and Hoole stood in the doorway. "Beetles!" Zak shouted. "They're everywhere!" He saw a beetle scuttle across the floor and stepped on it—forgetting he wasn't wearing shoes. There was a *crack!* as its shell was crushed, and then Zak felt squishy stuff spread across the bottom of his foot.

Tash didn't know whether to laugh or scream in horror.

The wriggling bugs reminded her of the horrible image of the murdered Imperial, but the sight of Zak dancing around his cabin scratching at his clothes was hilarious. "Zak, I thought we weren't supposed to kill any drog beetles!"

"Tell *them* that!" he cried, plucking the last beetle from the inside of his shirt collar. He tossed it against the wall. The beetle thudded against the wall and fell to the cabin floor. Stunned, it turned first one way, then the other. By the time it started to scurry away, Zak had crushed it with the end of his skimboard.

When all the beetles were dead, Zak gave one enormous, disgusted shudder and sat down.

"That was not prime," he breathed.

"How did they get in here?" Tash wondered, carefully avoiding dead beetle bodies as she stepped into the room.

"More importantly," Hoole added, "*why* did they come in here? These creatures have no reason to crawl onboard the ship." He considered. "Curious. First thing tomorrow morning, we will go see Vroon. Perhaps he can tell us something. In the meantime, as long as you are in no real danger, I suggest we all get some rest."

No real danger, Zak thought. *Try telling yourself that when you've got little creepy-crawlies under your blanket.*

Tash helped Zak sweep the remains of the drog beetles from his cabin and change his bed covers. But once he was back in bed again, Zak couldn't sleep.

"I should have told everyone that first day," he said out loud. "I should have told them I'd broken the law and

57

killed a shreev. It was an accident. It's just like with the engines. I should have told them." He scratched his head furiously—it still felt like there were bugs crawling through it. "But how do I tell everyone now? I'd have to admit that I tried to cover it up!"

Zak finally fell asleep, his dreams alternating between images of the swarming beetles and the disappointed face of Uncle Hoole once he found out about the shreev. Zak didn't know which was worse.

Zak slept in late the next day. By the time he stumbled out of bed, rubbing his cheeks to wake up, Tash and Hoole were dressed and ready.

"Hurry, please," Uncle Hoole insisted. "I would like to speak with Vroon about these insects, and then depart as soon as possible."

Zak looked hopeful. "Are the engines fixed?"

"Almost," his uncle replied. "Another hour or two of work should do it."

As soon as Zak was dressed they left the *Shroud* together and headed toward Vroon's workshop.

Except for Thrawn's shuttle, the Imperials had left, but the evidence of their presence was everywhere. Deep gouges had been cut out of the thick grass, and entire flower patches had been trampled.

"This is exactly what I had feared," Hoole said, a hint of sadness creeping into his even voice. "This garden is hundreds, perhaps thousands of years old. In one day, the Empire has destroyed part of it. Imagine what would happen if the Imperials took permanent control of the planet. That is why a complete record of the Sikadian Gardens must be made and preserved.''

''Uncle Hoole. I just thought of something,'' Tash said. ''Do you think there's some connection between the Empire and these beetles? We were here for a full day without any real problems. But the minute the Empire showed up, the bugs seemed to be everywhere. Zak found one in his food right when they arrived, they were all over that dead Imperial, and then they swarmed into Zak's cabin. Maybe it's an Imperial plot.''

No it isn't, Zak thought. *It's just me.*

But he still couldn't bring himself to say it out loud.

They reached Vroon's workshop. The door was ajar, so Hoole tapped on it lightly. There was no answer.

''Hello!'' Hoole called out, but still no one responded.

Hoole pushed the door open, then jumped back, startled.

Zak could see just inside the workshop around the edge of Hoole's arm. He saw the workbenches and the tables. He saw the plant wired to its digital readout. And he saw Vroon sitting on the floor.

Buried beneath a swarming mound of beetles.

CHAPTER 9

Vroon's body was nearly covered with a layer of drog beetles three or four deep. The beetles were crawling all over him, but very slowly. Unlike the beetles they had found on the dead Imperial, or the beetles that had swarmed on Zak's bed, these bugs did not move in frantic, scurrying motions. They waddled slowly around Vroon's body like little old men waking up from a nap.

Zak became aware of a soft sound filling the workshop. It was a low, steady hum. It was so sweet and soothing that Zak began to yawn.

"Is he—?" Tash whispered.

"No," Hoole replied softly. "Listen to that sound. It's wingsong. Vroon is using wingsong to influence the beetles."

"How can he stand having them crawl all over him like that!" Zak wondered. "It's disgusting."

They watched for a few more minutes, transfixed, as Vroon continued to soothe the beetles. Slowly, however, the wingsong started to wear off. The beetles seemed to become more agitated, moving in faster circles, hopping and leaping over one another.

Then Vroon shook his entire body. All at once, the beetles spread their wings, and the swarm lifted away from Vroon like a cloud. He slipped out from beneath them as the drog beetles settled onto the floor.

Only then did Vroon notice his visitors. "What do you want?"

"That was astonishing," Hoole observed.

Vroon picked up a net and began to scoop up the beetles, depositing them into the glass container Zak had seen before. "I have been doing communication experiments with the drog beetles, just as I have with plants. I've found that these elegant creatures are soothed by the sound of wingsong."

"How could you stand having them crawl all over you like that?" Zak asked. "I mean, they're *disgus* . . ." His voice trailed off as he realized what he was saying, and who he was saying it to.

Vroon's forelegs twitched. "Beauty is in the eye of the beholder."

"Vroon, we have a question for you," Hoole asked, getting to the point. "Last night a swarm of these beetles crawled into our ship—"

"And all over my bed!" Zak interjected.

"You didn't harm them, did you?" Vroon nearly shrieked.

Hoole blinked. "Unfortunately, there was no other way to eliminate the problem."

The caretaker spun away, rubbing his forearms across his triangular head in a soothing motion, muttering, "No, no, no. This is terrible! Tragic!"

"I apologize for any damage we've done to the beetle population," Hoole said. "But we have seen so many beetles, I was wondering if possibly there has already been some imbalance in the system."

Zak held his breath. This was it. Vroon would discover that there weren't enough shreevs to eat all the drog beetles. They would discover that one of the shreevs had been killed. He felt his heart pound against his chest. He should have learned his lesson. He should have told Uncle Hoole right away.

Instead, Vroon replied, "There is no imbalance!"

Zak was astonished. *Could I have been wrong about the shreev? Maybe it was only stunned. Maybe I've been worried for nothing.*

Or maybe, he considered, *Vroon just hasn't noticed the imbalance yet. Maybe it takes more than a few days for the beetle population to expand.*

Zak didn't know which theory was correct. What he did

know was that his stomach had suddenly tied itself up in knots. Now was his chance to come clean and confess what he'd done.

But hadn't he wanted to handle this problem himself? And hadn't the problem gone away? If there was no imbalance in the garden, then why should Zak tell anyone he'd killed a shreev? He would just get into trouble over nothing.

For the first time, it occurred to Zak that he could actually get away absolutely free. He didn't have to tell anyone. Uncle Hoole and Tash would never know he'd broken a law.

Zak wasn't sure he liked the way that made him feel.

Vroon finished netting all the drog beetles and dropping them back into their container. Hoole said to him, "You are the caretaker of this garden and I assume you know your business, but are you quite certain that there hasn't been an accident? Perhaps some shreevs have taken ill. There have been several incidents—"

"The swarm in your ship is easily explained," Vroon said abruptly. Although he continued to talk to Hoole, Zak could see that the caretaker wasn't really paying attention. Vroon was staring into the glass case, never taking his eyes off the beetles in his collection. "The drog beetles are attracted to warmth, especially when they are preparing to lay their eggs. Since your ship is made of metal—a material unnatural to this area, I might add—it undoubtedly grew hot in the sun. The drog beetles were attracted by the heat and crawled inside to make nests."

"They were going to lay eggs in my bed?" Zak nearly choked. The image of drog beetle larvae squirming around in his sheets made him gag.

"Most likely," Vroon relied. "It is nesting season for the drog beetles right now. They're probably looking for good sites, that's all. Hardly an incident worth recording."

Hoole considered. "Perhaps you're right. But these beetles did seem quite . . . aggressive."

Vroon nodded vigorously. His voice grew more excited with each word. "Indeed. They get that way in large groups, especially during the nesting season. In ones and twos they are docile and hardly move. But the more beetles there are, the more aggressive they become. A swarm of them might even—" he stopped. "Well, it doesn't matter what a swarm of them might do. After all, the shreevs keep the population down."

"Are you sure?" said a new voice.

It was Sh'shak. The other S'krrr had entered as Vroon was speaking. "I walked from the far end of the garden to get here. On the way I noticed a great many beetles everywhere. I thought you would want to know, Vroon."

"I have everything under control!" the caretaker snapped. "I know my job. Everything is exactly as it should be."

"Not quite," came yet another voice.

General Thrawn entered the small building holding a blaster in his hand. Lieutenant Tier followed him, toting a powerful blaster rifle.

"What's the meaning of this!" Vroon sputtered. "This is my workshop!"

"This does not concern you, Vroon," Thrawn said. He leveled his blaster at Sh'shak. "Sh'shak of the S'krrr, you are under arrest. The charge is murder. The sentence is death."

CHAPTER

10

They were aboard the Imperial shuttle *Tessera,* the craft Thrawn had landed right inside the garden. Thrawn and his lieutenant had insisted that Zak, Tash, and Hoole accompany him as he marched Sh'shak back to his ship. Once they arrived, binders were placed on Sh'shak's wrists.

"Under my Imperial authority," Thrawn explained to his captive. "I could have shot you down where you stood. But I believe in following procedure whenever possible, so I've brought you here to record the evidence against you, and to allow you to make a statement if you so desire. These three," Thrawn said, waving to Zak, Tash, and Hoole, "will serve as witnesses of the evidence against you."

Thrawn nodded to his lieutenant, and Tier switched on a small recording device. Thrawn stated his name and rank, and Sh'shak's name, then asked, "Do you confess to the murder of Lieutenant Wolver yesterday?"

"No, I am innocent," Sh'shak replied calmly.

"Then how do you explain this?" Thrawn demanded. He walked over to a storage cabinet and removed the weapon Zak and Tash had seen Sh'shak use the day before. "For the record, I am holding a vibropike of the kind used on S'krrr," Thrawn stated. "This pike was discovered hidden in some bushes inside the garden. We scanned the pike for fibers and skin samples. This pike definitely belongs to you." Thrawn leaned forward. "And it could easily have been used to kill my officer."

"Uncle Hoole, what should we do?" Tash whispered.

"Nothing," her uncle replied in a barely audible voice.

Sh'shak spoke up. "I do not deny that this is my weapon. But I did not kill anyone. You say you examined the weapon. Did you find any of the lieutenant's blood on it?"

Thrawn shrugged. "You could easily have cleaned the blade of the weapon to remove such evidence. Besides," the Imperial captain added, "what would a so-called poet need with the weapon of a killer?"

"On S'krrr," Sh'shak replied, "the most respected of our artists are poet-warriors—individuals who have mastered both the good side and the dark side of their personalities. We strike a balance, just as this garden strikes a balance. I have the honor of being recognized by my people as both a poet and a warrior."

"A convenient story," Thrawn countered, "especially for someone whose false identity has just been revealed."

Hoole found his chance to speak up. "It's true. You only have to look at the culture of the S'krrr. I have spent quite a bit of time over the last few days talking with Sh'shak and studying the S'krrr beliefs. Their history is full of both beauty and violence. So it is no surprise they have become both artists and warriors. They learn to fight with traditional weapons, and they perform ritual combats. It is part of their culture."

Tash suddenly remembered her conversation with Thrawn. "Captain Thrawn, you said almost the same thing yourself when you were walking through the garden."

Thrawn considered. "Perhaps. But even if this is true, and Sh'shak has a reason for carrying a deadly weapon near Imperial personnel, it still doesn't mean he's innocent." The Imperial captain glanced at a small datapad. "My medical staff determined that Lieutenant Wolver's death occurred at approximately six o'clock in the morning. Where were you at that time?"

Sh'shak paused. "I was in the garden."

Thrawn nodded. "And what were you doing?"

Again, Sh'shak paused. Zak wondered what Sh'shak would say next. If he told the truth, it might seal his fate. And somewhere in the back of his mind, Zak wondered what *he* would do in the same situation.

Finally, Sh'shak said, "I was practicing with my vibropike."

A brief, thin smile crossed Thrawn's face again. "I see. So you were in the location of the murder, with a weapon that could have caused the murder. And yet you say you're innocent."

Sh'shak nodded. "That is correct."

"It's true!" Zak blurted out. He wanted to help Sh'shak. The S'krrr had told the truth, even though it made him seem guilty. It wasn't fair to let him stand alone. "Tash and I saw him. He was practicing on a little tree."

Thrawn blinked his red eyes once. "Ah, yes. You two were also in the garden that morning," he said to Zak and Tash. "What were you doing there?"

Zak decided to speak for himself and his sister. He also decided to follow Sh'shak's example and tell the truth. "We were following someone from your shuttle," he admitted. "It was probably Lieutenant Wolver, but we couldn't see clearly through the mist."

The Imperial captain turned squarely toward Zak and Tash. Then he looked at Hoole. "Simple tourists do not follow Imperial officers. Your involvement in this affair grows deeper—"

"That seems to happen wherever we go," Zak muttered under his breath.

"—and I'm beginning to wonder just who you are," Thrawn concluded. "As soon as we have finished with this S'krrr, I'll have you three taken to my Star Destroyer for identification."

Zak and Tash swallowed. Once Thrawn looked into their

past, he'd find out they were wanted by none other than Darth Vader. But there was nothing they could do as long as Thrawn and his aide had them covered with their blasters.

"In the meantime," Thrawn said, turning back to Sh'shak, "I have no intention of killing an Imperial citizen without a good reason. And the claims of these children are easy enough to verify." The blue-skinned officer pointed toward the shuttle's exit. "Show me where you practiced. If there's evidence that you were actually there during the murder, your life may be spared."

A few moments later they were walking single file through the garden. Zak and Tash led the way, with Hoole behind them. Sh'shak followed Hoole, and Thrawn and Lieutenant Tier brought up the rear, blasters in hand.

Now and then, Zak glanced back at Uncle Hoole. The Shi'ido's expression was stonier and more unreadable than ever. Zak knew that Hoole was preparing to make a move. There were only two Imperials—even though they were armed—and with his shape-changing powers, Hoole could probably overcome them both.

"Lieutenant Tier," Captain Thrawn said as they marched. "It occurs to me that there is a wild card in this sabacc deck, and I dislike wild cards. The caretaker, Vroon, is not under surveillance."

"That's true, Captain," Lieutenant Tier said. "But you don't suppose that gardener could have—?"

"I suppose nothing," Thrawn interrupted. "I simply want to have all points covered. Go find Vroon and bring him to me."

With a quick salute, Lieutenant Tier marched away and headed back toward the caretaker's workshop.

Now, if there were trouble, the odds were in Hoole's favor.

Zak and Tash saw the small hill up ahead. They reached it quickly. At the top stood the small sapling, still marked with the cuts of Sh'shak's weapon. The grass around the tree was torn and chopped up by the quick movements of the S'krrr's feet.

"There's your evidence," Tash said. "This is where we found Sh'shak yesterday morning."

Now that he was alone among civilians, Thrawn moved more cautiously. He kept a safe distance from the others, and he spared only a quick glance at the tree and the ground. But that glance told him all he needed to know. "It seems the S'krrr was here," he agreed.

Zak gave an audible sigh.

"However," the Imperial captain continued, "there is nothing to indicate how long you were here, or what time. For all I know you practiced on this tree, then slaughtered Lieutenant Wolver and left him for the beetles to eat."

"But that is not the case," Sh'shak insisted.

Thrawn shrugged. "I am making my decision based on the evidence at hand. That evidence suggests you're the killer."

He pointed his blaster at Sh'shak's chest.

"Aggghghhh!"

A strangled cry flew up the hill to meet them. It was followed a second later by Lieutenant Tier. The Imperial aide stumbled to the crest of the hill, gagging and choking on something. His blaster was gone. His eyes were wild with fear, and he clutched at his throat.

"Tier, explain yourself," Thrawn ordered. "What's wrong?"

Lieutenant Tier opened his mouth to speak, but instead of words, a swarm of drog beetles spilled from his mouth.

CHAPTER

Lieutenant Tier collapsed. His body twisted and turned as more drog beetles poured out of his mouth. They were also inside his clothes and crawling in his hair.

Seconds later the officer stopped moving. The beetles continued to crawl over his body. Zak was too horrified to go near another beetle-covered body, but from a distance, it looked like the insects were biting into Lieutenant Tier's skin. He remembered something Vroon had told him: The drog beetles would eat anything. No, not anything—*everything*.

Hoole and Sh'shak knelt beside the body, flicking beetles away, but it was useless. The officer was dead.

"How—how did he die?" Tash asked unsteadily. "Was it . . . Is it? I mean . . ."

"It seems quite obvious now," Thrawn said. He studied

73

the air, looking for signs of danger. "When we found the first body, we naturally assumed that someone had murdered Lieutenant Wolver and left his body lying on the ground, where the drog beetles found it."

"But that is not the case," said Sh'shak.

"No," Hoole agreed. "It is far worse than that. The drog beetles are killing people."

Hoole's statement hit Zak like a blaster bolt. *The beetles are killing people.* Vroon had said that the beetles became more aggressive in large numbers . . . and their numbers had grown because he had killed a shreev. In a way, *he* had killed the two Imperials.

"It's all my fault!" The words burst out of him. "Everything is all my fault." He felt a hot tear spring into his eye and he tried to squeeze it away.

All eyes turned to him. Hoole stood up from the body and said, "Zak, what are you talking about?"

The confession that Zak should have made days ago poured out of him. "Uncle Hoole, I really messed up. The first day we got here, I went for a walk. A shreev attacked me. It was probably only hunting a drog beetle that had landed on my hand, but I didn't know that. I thought it was after *me,* and I hit it with a stick. I killed it. Then, when I found out it was against the law to kill shreevs, I didn't tell anyone. I didn't want to get into trouble."

"I see," Hoole said.

"I thought I could fix the problem myself," Zak

moaned. "Just like with the ship. I should have known better, but I figured that if I could just kill as many beetles as a shreev every day, I wouldn't upset the balance of nature. But then the Imperials showed up, and we found the body, and I didn't follow my plan. And now the beetles are everywhere. It's all my fault."

"Ridiculous," Thrawn snorted.

"What?" Zak asked. He was expecting everyone to be angry. Instead, Thrawn scoffed at him.

"Your theory is simply wrong," the Imperial stated. "This garden covers dozens of kilometers. It's probably home to thousands of shreevs and even more thousands of beetles. The idea that the loss of one shreev could cause such a drastic increase is simply ridiculous. It does not calculate."

"No, it's true!" Zak insisted. "That's how delicate things are in this place. Sh'shak, even you said so."

Sh'shak's wings fluttered thoughtfully. "I said that was the legend. I am not sure the truth is quite so clear cut."

"One thing *is* clear," Thrawn said as he holstered his blaster. "You are not the murderer, Sh'shak. You are free to go." He removed the binders from Sh'shak's arms.

"Now what?" Tash asked.

"I do not think we are in any immediate danger," Hoole guessed. "We have dealt with the drog beetles before. We should get back to the ship as soon as possible, but I think we should stop by Vroon's workshop first. Maybe the care-taker can explain the population increase.''

''This garden is his responsibility. He has some explain-ing to do,'' Thrawn growled. ''Two of my men have died here.''

They walked quickly. The idea of being smothered to death by beetles made them hurry—even Thrawn moved with a quick step. They kept seeing small clouds of drog beetles take flight and buzz through the air. Each swarm they saw was bigger than the last.

''I'm surprised Vroon would have let things get so out of control,'' Sh'shak commented. ''He has been taking care of this garden for years.''

''How could he know?'' Zak said miserably. Despite what Thrawn had said, he still felt guilty.

They arrived at Vroon's workshop a few moments later and burst in without knocking. Startled, Vroon looked up from his work. He was leaning over the container of bee-tles, and Zak had a weird feeling that, seconds before, Vroon had been whispering to them.

''What's the meaning of this?'' the caretaker demanded. ''You can't just barge in here. I am working.''

''We have no time for pleasantries,'' Thrawn snapped. ''Two of my men have died in your garden, and I think those beetles had something to do with it.''

''Vroon,'' Hoole said in a more gentle voice, ''as we said before, the drog beetle population is growing. We've only been here a few days and we've seen it. They'll soon take over the Sikadian Garden if you don't find a way to destroy them."

Vroon recoiled as if someone had struck him. He nearly shrieked, "Destroy them? Destroy them! I can't destroy them. They're my family!"

CHAPTER

Vroon put his body between the others and the container of beetles in his workshop. "Don't you understand?" he cried. "The drog beetles are the ancestors of the S'krrr. We evolved from them. We can't kill them. They're . . . they're beautiful!"

"Oh, no," Zak groaned. "Somehow I think they put the wrong person in charge of the garden."

"Vroon," Sh'shak said, "while it's true that—"

"I have no time for this," Thrawn interrupted harshly. "All life evolved from earlier life. That is basic scientific knowledge. But you don't see other species worshipping insects."

"We are different," Vroon insisted. His wings fluttered gently and he pointed to Sh'shak. "We can communicate with our ancestors through wingsong. I've done it, Sh'shak. I've learned to speak with them. There is so much they can teach us!''

Sh'shak nodded. "It is an interesting thought. Perhaps we can take your idea to our leaders. But that is no reason to let the beetles overrun the planet. Some of them must be destroyed. And you must help us do it.''

"No!" Vroon cried.

"Then you are under arrest," Thrawn declared, drawing his blaster, "for the murder of two Imperial officers.''

"No!" Vroon repeated. He dove for one of the open windows. Thrawn fired, but the S'krrr was too fast. He was out the window and scurrying out of sight.

"We must follow," Sh'shak said, dashing for the door.

The others followed as quickly as possible, but none of them could move as fast as Sh'shak. Zak could see why the S'krrr had become warriors as well as poets. Sh'shak had gone in a moment from complete stillness to blinding speed.

"We can't lose sight of him!" Thrawn growled. He was starting to outpace the others, and it was obvious that the Imperial captain had kept himself in top physical condition. "He knows the garden too well. We'll never find him!"

"We have to," Sh'shak called back without slowing. "He's the only one who knows how badly the garden's been damaged. He's the only one who will know how to save it!"

Zak, Tash, Hoole, and Thrawn soon lost sight of Vroon, but they could still see Sh'shak in pursuit, and they followed his lead.

Thrawn had been right. Vroon knew every centimeter of the Sikadian Garden, and he did everything he could to lose them. He ran through thick brambles, he plunged into thick clumps of trees and bushes, and he scrambled up and down the sides of steep ravines. But Sh'shak was able to keep up with him, and as long as they kept him in sight, they thought they still had a chance.

Finally, they ran into a small forest of tall, pale-barked trees and found Sh'shak standing in the middle of the path. A slight breeze blew through the forest, making the tree leaves stir and rustle. Though he had run farther and faster than any of them, the S'krrr was hardly breathing hard.

"D-Did you lose him?" Zak panted.

"I am afraid so," Sh'shak replied. "But that is not why I stopped. I am afraid we have a much more immediate problem. I suggest we abandon our attempt to find Vroon, and try to save ourselves."

"What do you mean?" Thrawn demanded.

Sh'shak pointed to first one tree, then another, and then another. Zak looked around. As his eyes adjusted to the dim light beneath the tree branches, he realized that the stirring and rustling he'd heard were not caused by any breeze. Every leaf on every branch of every tree was covered with beetles.

Thousands of them.

Millions of them.

"This is not right," Sh'shak insisted. "This cannot be due to the loss of one shreev. At their fastest rate, the beetles could not reproduce this much in three days, even if a thousand shreevs had been killed."

"Make no sudden moves," Hoole said quietly. "We know the beetles become more aggressive in large numbers. A small swarm of them attacked and killed a full-grown human. Who knows what this many might try?"

Tash sniffed. "What's that smell? It's disgusting."

The stench drifted through a break in the trees to their right. Moving slowly and trying not to breathe through their noses, they stepped through the opening and found themselves in a small clearing. In the center of the clearing was a deep pit.

The pit was filled with the bodies of shreevs. Armies of beetles covered the pit, eating the creatures that usually ate them.

"There must be hundreds of shreevs in there," Tash whispered.

"Thousands," Sh'shak said, bowing his head. "Vroon has been at his work for some time, it seems."

Tash frowned. "Does this mean we won't be able to save the garden?"

"It's no longer the garden I'm worried about," Sh'shak said. "We must hurry."

Turning, they made their way out of the beetle-infested forest. If Zak hadn't been so frightened of the creeping insects that scurried underfoot and flew overhead, he would have been relieved. As they walked out of the forest, with the bright sun of S'krrr shining down on the garden, Zak told himself that the shreev he had killed hadn't been the start of this whole mess. At least that was something.

But Sh'shak's next statement wiped out his relief. "If Vroon has been tampering with the natural balance in the garden for even one year, that would be enough time for every female drog beetle to lay hundreds of eggs. And each of those young beetles would in turn hatch hundreds. That means this is not a small overpopulation problem. It means the garden could be infested with millions upon millions of beetles."

As if to emphasize the gloom in Sh'shak's words, a cloud passed over the sun.

"I have had enough of this garden," Thrawn said. "I'll summon a few gunboats to come down and scan the entire area." The Imperial reached for his comlink, but it was gone. "Blast," he muttered. "It must have fallen during the chase."

The sky grew suddenly darker. Zak looked up to see if storm clouds were moving in.

But the sky was not filled with storm clouds.

It was filled with beetles!

CHAPTER

The swarm of beetles spun like a tornado, and began to twist down out of the sky toward them.

"Look out!" Zak cried. But it was useless. The swarm was moving too quickly, and there was nowhere to run.

Suddenly, Hoole began to shiver, and the skin crawled across his bones. An instant later, a dark-winged shreev stood in his place.

"By the Emperor!" Thrawn cried. Then he paused and muttered, "A Shi'ido. How very interesting."

Hoole, in the shape of a shreev, launched himself into the air and darted directly at the massive swarm. Zak heard the shreev shriek as it plunged toward the cloud of hungry beetles.

It worked. Instinctively, the beetles swerved away from

their natural enemy. The entire cloud veered to the right, heading away from those still on the ground.

"This is our chance. Run!" Sh'shak urged.

"Where?" Zak asked.

"My ship," Thrawn ordered. "We'll be safe there."

"We won't have much time," Tash said.

She was right. Hoole in shreev form plunged into the cloud, striking at the thick wall of beetles. But one shreev could hardly attack the entire swarm. Although the beetles gave way wherever the shreev flew, the rest of the cloud leaked around it and continued to pour through the sky toward the victims on the ground.

Hoole was nearly overwhelmed by advancing beetles. Letting out one more frustrated shriek, he turned and flapped away. But instead of flying toward Zak and Tash, Hoole flew off in the opposite direction.

"Where's he going?" Zak called out as he started to run.

"Tactical retreat," Thrawn suggested. "Either that or he's a coward."

"Uncle Hoole is no coward!" Tash snapped.

Thrawn shrugged. "Either way, your Shi'ido friend won't be helping us now. We've got to get to the shuttle."

It was like racing the wind. Zak willed his feet to fly as fast as they could carry him as Thrawn and Sh'shak pulled ahead. Behind him, he could hear a soft *whirrr* sound grow into an angry buzz. And then the buzz became a violent drone.

The swarm was getting closer.

The sun vanished. Zak found himself running in near darkness, hoping he wouldn't trip over any stray rocks or clumps of grass.

The swarm was directly overhead.

"There's the shuttle!" Tash gasped.

Zak felt something bump against his ear. He swatted away a beetle that had landed on his shoulder. The fastest of the insects had reached them. A hail of bugs flew down on them from the sky.

Sh'shak and Thrawn had reached the shuttle and hurried up the ramp on the underside of the craft. As soon as he was inside, the Imperial turned and slapped something on the wall. The ramp began to rise.

"Hey!" Zak and Tash shouted.

Thrawn was going to lock them out!

CHAPTER

14

The ramp lifted off the ground.

"We're not going to make it," Zak moaned.

"Yes, we are," Tash encouraged. "Jump!"

Together they leaped for the rising ramp. Zak managed to catch hold of the edge by his fingertips. Tash grabbed hold, too, but her fingers quickly started to slip.

"Help!" she shouted.

Zak let go with one hand and grabbed hold of her tunic. "Gotcha. Climb up!"

The ramp was halfway closed.

Tash scrambled over the edge and onto the ramp itself, then hauled her brother up. They collapsed, grateful to be inside as the ramp sealed itself shut.

Outside, they heard *thud! thud! thud!* as hundreds of beetles battered themselves against the hull of the shuttle.

Tash and Zak struggled to their feet and stumbled toward the cockpit, where Thrawn had just dropped into the pilot's seat.

"You tried to leave us out there!" Tash shouted at him.

"Tactical decision," Thrawn explained coldly. "Waiting for you might have allowed the swarm to get into the ship. I would have done the same thing if you were my men."

"Well, we're *not* your men!" Zak snapped.

Thrawn spared him a brief, disdainful glare. "Be grateful. If you were, I would have ordered you to stand outside and delay the swarm until I had secured the ship."

Thrawn began to flip switches on the shuttle's control panel.

"What are you doing?" Sh'shak asked.

"Evacuating," Thrawn explained.

Zak and Tash yelled together: "You can't!"

"The Shi'ido is still out there somewhere," Sh'shak observed. "He saved our lives."

Thrawn hardly paused. "And I'm grateful. I assume he can take care of himself. If not, those are the fortunes of war. But we must retreat before—" He flipped a switch. "Blast!"

There was no power. Thrawn tried several backup units, and still he could get no power to the controls. "The com-link's dead, too," he said, checking the communications station. "I have no way of calling for help."

Thrawn pushed past them and headed back for the engine room. The others followed. Their footsteps on the shuttle's metal floor banged almost as loudly as the sound of drog beetles thumping against the ship.

Thrawn pried open the maintenance hatch, exposing the main generators, and jumped back in surprise. A dozen beetles lifted off the cables, fluttering in the air. They could see dozens more crawling in and out of the wire systems. Several of the bugs had been fried by crossed circuits, and sparks flew from their crisped bodies.

"They've shorted out everything," Zak said. "Your whole power supply is shot."

"Which makes this ship as dead as ours," Tash said.

Thrawn replaced the maintenance panel. Although Thrawn was far colder and crueler, he reminded Zak of Hoole. Even in the midst of chaos, with a swarm of hungry beetles trying to reach them and a ship that had gone dead, Thrawn remained calm and collected.

The Imperial ordered them to retreat to the shuttle's small lounge area. "We can't move, but at least we're protected," he observed. "Eventually, when the *Vengeance* realizes we have lost contact, they'll send reinforcements down to look for me. Then we'll be able to leave. In the meantime, we should be safe."

"What about the air vents?" Zak asked.

"The vents?" Thrawn repeated.

Zak's heart slammed against his ribs. "Standard procedure. Open the air vents on landing in a breathable atmosphere.''

''The vents!'' Thrawn cursed.

They looked up at a tiny grill set in the wall of the lounge, just as beetles began to pour through the opening.

CHAPTER 15

The crawling drog beetles spread out like a dark stain along the wall of the room. The only tall person in the room, Thrawn tore a cushion from a seat and shoved it against the vent. But it did no good—beetles continued to wiggle their way under and around the soft cushion.

Behind Thrawn, Zak, Tash, and Sh'shak tried to fight off the insects. Sh'shak moved with a combination of lightning speed and perfect grace, swatting beetles right out of the air.

Tash found a clipboard on a table top and used it as a shield and weapon, slapping the insects out of her way.

Zak tried to say something, but as he opened his mouth to speak, a beetle flew right into his mouth and clung to his tongue. Gagging, he spit the bug out of his mouth. He pulled his tunic up over his head to keep the insects out of his hair and eyes, but when he did, more landed on his exposed stomach and started to crawl up his body.

"Agghhh!" he cried, slapping them away. The beetles swarmed so thickly in the small room that he could simply swing his arms and strike a half dozen, stunning them to the ground. He swung his arms and stomped his feet, hoping to kill as many as possible.

"We cannot stay here!" Sh'shak cried out. "We'll be buried alive!"

"Agreed," Thrawn grunted. "This shuttle has become a death trap."

"What about your ship?" Sh'shak asked the Arrandas as he slapped more beetles out of the air.

"Same problem," Zak replied, trying not to open his mouth too wide. "The air vents will be open. And we need to make a few more repairs."

Thrawn snatched up a second cushion and tried to stuff it against the air vent. "That leaves only Vroon's workshop."

"Bad idea!" Tash said. She shuddered as she felt a large beetle crawl across her neck. She managed to grab it before it scrambled down the back of her shirt. "There's no trans-parasteel in the windows."

"But the walls are made of stone," Thrawn countered. "And I think the wooden roof will hold for a while. There are workbenches and tables we can use to seal up the window openings."

Zak killed another beetle, but it was like slapping at the ocean—more beetles just filled the vacant space. "It can't be any worse than staying here!"

As a group they retreated toward the hatchway again. Outside, they could still hear thousands and thousands of beetles bump against the hull as they swirled around the shuttle.

Zak caught Sh'shak and Thrawn speaking warrior-to-warrior. "You know," Sh'shak observed, "the odds of survival are not good."

Thrawn nodded. "But I prefer to die trying. Let's go."

Since the power was out, Thrawn used a manual control switch to lower the ramp. Once it was lowered, it could not be raised again until the ship was repaired. "There's no turning back," he said. Then he plunged into the storm of insects.

Sh'shak followed, and then Zak and Tash. Taking a deep breath so he wouldn't have to open his mouth to breathe for at least a few moments, Zak charged down the ramp, expecting to run into a swirling wall of beetles.

To his surprise, he felt nothing. The beetles had turned their attention to the shuttle, and because the ramp was built on the bottom of the craft, they were actually running *beneath* the swarm. Momentarily free of the crawling, scratching bugs, Zak ran so fast that he almost caught up with Sh'shak and Thrawn. Tash was only a half-step behind.

But the movement of four figures on the ground caught

the attention of the hungry swarm. A few hundred drog beetles massed together had become aggressive enough to attack a human. Now a few *million* whirred overhead, ready to attack anything that moved. The cloud plunged like a giant buzzing spear toward the four runners.

"We're . . . not going . . . to make it," Zak panted.

"Wait!" Tash cried. "Look!"

Another dark cloud appeared. This one was ahead of them and closing in fast. For a second Zak thought he saw even more beetles, but then he realized that this cloud was different. Within the cloud he could see the flapping of hundreds of wings, and instead of droning angrily, this dark shadow shrieked as it moved across the sky.

It was flock of shreevs.

They came by the hundreds, shrieking and diving into the swarm of beetles. The two dark clouds collided, and the shreevs broke through the wall of beetles like a battering ram. The beetle swarm shivered, and suddenly came apart. Smaller clouds veered this way and that, fleeing the shreevs that tried to eat them.

One of the shreevs broke off from the main flock and streaked toward Zak and Tash. At the last possible moment, the shreev pulled out of a steep dive and landed on the ground. Then before their eyes the shreev's body quivered and expanded outward, until it had changed into the figure of Uncle Hoole.

CHAPTER 16

Tash and Zak threw their arms around their uncle.

"Are we glad to see you!" Zak cried.

Thrawn nodded admiringly. "A fine strategy. How did you think of it?"

Hoole shrugged. "It became apparent that one shreev would not halt the swarm for long, so I flew off in search of other shreevs. I hoped that by rousing them, I could get them to hunt."

Sh'shak watched the skies. Shreevs swooped and dove in all directions, feasting on the thick, helpless clouds of beetles. "They seem to be making the most of their meal."

"They are welcome to it," Hoole said. A look of mild disgust crossed his face as he wiped his mouth. "Believe me, I have eaten my fill."

Tash explained what had happened aboard the shuttle, but Zak was no longer paying attention. He stared at the sky. There were still plenty of shreevs hunting the beetles, but something Sh'shak had said bothered him. He hardly listened as Tash explained that Thrawn's ship had been damaged by the beetle infestation, and that they were making their way to Vroon's workshop.

"But now that you have broken up the swarm," Thrawn suggested, "perhaps we should simply return to my shuttle and make repairs. Then we can fly to safety."

Zak shook his head. Something was wrong. The shreevs were slowing down. *They're making the most of their meal,* Sh'shak had said.

Zak saw several shreevs break away and fly heavily, lazily toward a grove of trees.

They're making the most of their meal . . .

More shreevs broke away, and suddenly Zak remembered. "We've got to hurry!" he shouted in alarm. "We don't have much time!"

Thrawn looked around for some new danger. "What do you mean?"

"The shreevs!" Zak said, pointing skyward. More of the dark flying creatures had broken off and were soaring away in search of a resting place. "Shreevs only hunt until they get their fill. Then they sleep off their full stomachs."

A deep frown sank into Hoole's long face. "And the

beetles by far outnumber the shreevs. There will still be hundreds of thousands of beetles left when all the shreevs have gone to take their naps."

Tash shuddered. "Which is more than enough to come after us."

Zak looked left, then right. One way led back to Thrawn's ship, the other toward Vroon's workshop. "Which way should we go?"

"To my ship," Thrawn ordered. "Now that we have time to work, I can make repairs."

"No—to the workshop," Hoole countered. "Vroon knows more about these insects than anyone alive. Perhaps there is a weapon, or some information in the cottage, that we can use."

Thrawn was in no position to argue. None of the others were Imperials, and no one else would follow him. They turned and hurried toward the workshop.

They were still a hundred meters from the old stone cottage when the last of the shreevs had flown away, leaving the sky still buzzing with beetles. At first, the insects continued to drift about in small clouds. But soon the clouds joined together, turning the hum of their wings into a louder buzz.

Anxiously, Zak, Tash, and the others started to run.

They reached the workshop just as the sun vanished behind the swarm.

They found the workshop door ajar. "Maybe Vroon came back," Zak said. "Now that his drog beetles are attacking everything in sight, maybe we can persuade him to help us."

They pushed the door open.

Just as Zak had hoped, Vroon was inside. But all that was left of him was his hard, transparent S'krrr shell. His eyes and the rest of his body had been eaten away.

CHAPTER

Beetles crawled in and out of Vroon's remains. More beetles fluttered around the workshop, and for a moment, Zak feared that the swarm had reached the building before them. Then he saw the glass container that had held Vroon's own collection. It had fallen to the floor and shattered.

"He must have come back for his collection," Zak guessed.

"So much for finding a weapon here," Thrawn scoffed. "If Vroon had anything to use against these beetles, it obviously didn't work against the swarm."

Quickly, the small group braced itself for the coming swarm of insects. While Zak and Tash busied themselves stomping on the beetles in the room, the others overturned tables and workbenches. Then, using tools in the workshop, they laid plastoid trays and tabletops—anything flat—

across the open windows, sealing them shut. Just as Thrawn slammed the door shut and jammed a bench behind it, the swarm struck the building.

Thuk! Thuk! Thuk!

Hard, tiny bodies smashed against the stone walls of the workshop. Alone, each beetle weighed almost nothing. But as hundreds of thousands of them slammed against the door and windows again and again, they acted like a battering ram. The walls were already starting to shake.

Zak looked around. "There's got to be something here we can use. Vroon was an expert on these beetles."

Thrawn scowled. "Vroon was insane. He worshipped bugs. He miscalculated and now he is dead. We must be careful not to miscalculate as well. Our best chance for survival is to wait it out until my ship notices I have not checked in. They will send down enough forces to wipe out ten million insects, and we'll be rid of these pests once and for all."

Zak, Tash, and Hoole exchanged glances. That might be *Thrawn's* best chance for survival, but for them it was like jumping out of the rancor's claws and right into its mouth. Once they were on board an Imperial Star Destroyer, they might never get off again.

As the walls continued to shiver and groan under the weight of untold numbers of beetles, Zak and Tash searched the workshop for anything they had missed—a weapon or a chemical, anything Vroon might have used to keep control over the beetles.

Zak knelt down and sifted through the piles of objects they had overturned earlier. He pulled aside a large plant, and found it connected by wires to a small digital device—the device Vroon had used to measure the plant's reactions.

He stared at the device so long and hard that Tash finally asked him, "You find something we can use?"

"No," he replied. "But I think I have an idea."

He held up the plant, wires and all. "You know, we're going about this the wrong way. This is Vroon's workshop. He spent a whole year destroying shreevs so his drog beetles could survive. We're not going to find anything here that will do them any harm. He would have gotten rid of it long ago."

"Right," Tash said, dropping a vial of water she'd hoped was some more dangerous chemical. "So what do we do?"

"We don't hurt the beetles, or scare them off," Zak said. "We try to communicate with them."

Tash shook her head and jabbed a finger at the wired plant Zak was holding. "You can't talk to all those beetles with this instrument."

"Not with this," Zak said. "With those!"

He pointed at Sh'shak. At Sh'shak's wings.

The three adults stopped their work. Sh'shak fluttered his wings gently, filling the room with a questioning *skrrrr* sound. "Pardon me?"

"We saw Vroon do it!" Zak said excitedly. "Vroon sat here with beetles all over his body. But they were calm.

None of them bit him, they didn't suffocate him. They weren't aggressive at all."

"I remind you," Thrawn insisted disdainfully, "that you are suggesting we follow the example of someone who has recently been eaten alive."

A wide, thin piece of plastoid that had been fastened across one of the windows cracked and bent inward. A hundred insects slipped into the room before Hoole pushed another piece of broken tabletop across the hole.

Just as he sealed the opening, something groaned overhead.

"The roof," Thrawn said. "The wood is sagging under the weight of the beetles."

They all looked up. The wooden beams creaked. No one spoke, but everyone imagined what would happen if the ceiling collapsed, dropping an avalanche of beetles onto their heads.

"Clearly, we cannot wait forever," Hoole said. "And I, too, saw Vroon's experiment. For a short time, he did have control over the beetles. The trouble was that it did not last. And against such a large, aggressive, swarm, I suspect it would work for an even shorter amount of time." He paused. "It is evident that the S'krrr evolved out of creatures very much like the beetles we see here. Therefore, it is possible that Vroon was actually communicating with them through wingsong."

Reluctantly, Thrawn added, "You may be correct. When

101

I first began studying the garden, I noticed several patterns in the arrangement of its various segments. At first I assumed that these patterns were random. But since then I've learned more. The patterns in the garden very closely match the patterns of the beetles when they're swarming."

"What do you mean?" Zak asked.

"I mean that, in a very simple way, the beetles and the S'krrr think alike," Thrawn concluded.

"You mean Vroon was right?" Tash asked. "The drog beetles really are the S'krrrs' ancestors?"

Hoole nodded in agreement. "Yes. In the same way a particular squid is the ancestor of the Calamari, and a certain tree-climber is the ancestor of the Wookiees." He turned to Sh'shak. "More importantly, it means that you may be able to communicate with them."

"I will try," Sh'shak agreed. "But I doubt I can make my wingsong heard over the droning of the swarm."

"You'll have help," Hoole said. The skin shivered over his bones, and he transformed into a S'krrr. His wings fluttered as he said in a S'krrr's soft voice, "I don't know your language, but I can copy whatever sound you make."

"What will we do once the swarm is calmed down?" Zak asked.

"Simple," Hoole replied. "While we are communicating with the beetles, you and Tash will walk quickly and quietly down the path to the *Shroud*. The ship is almost fixed. You will finish the repairs and fly the ship back here to save us."

"You want us to *what*?" Tash gasped.

"Walk out there?" Zak echoed. He looked down at the shell that had once been Vroon. He wondered if the beetles would gnaw at *his* skeleton.

"Zak, Tash," Hoole said. He looked down at them understandingly. "I cannot—I would not—*make* you do this. But you may be our only chance. If I stay here to help Sh'shak, you are the only ones who can fix the ship."

Zak looked at his sister and knew what she was thinking. After all the times Hoole had saved them, how could they refuse him now? Zak said, "I—I think I can finish the ship pretty quickly. Especially if Captain Thrawn agrees to help."

"I agree to nothing," the Imperial retorted. "The entire venture still sounds foolish to me. If you are fortunate enough to calm this swarm down, I intend to return to my own ship and fix my comlink as quickly as possible."

Hoole's S'krrr wings fluttered irritably. "Very well. Let us begin."

Sh'shak seated himself in a comfortable place and took in a deep breath. Then softly, his wings began to stir. At first they could hear nothing but the familiar *skrrrr*. But slowly, over the *thuk! thuk! thuk!* of swarming beetles outside, the sound of his vibrating wings rose higher, filling the room and filtering out of the workshop to the garden beyond.

Once Sh'shak's wingsong had reached a steady pattern, Hoole joined in, imitating the S'krrr perfectly. The sound

103

of their wings was now so loud that Zak wanted to cover his ears, but so beautiful that he wanted to listen.

Outside, the drone of the swarm grew quieter.

As the song continued, Hoole signaled to Zak.

Hoping that the song had worked, Zak took a deep breath and opened the door.

And instantly vanished behind a cloud of swarming beetles.

CHAPTER

18

Zak dared not open his mouth to call for help. If he had, he would have breathed in a lungful of insects. But just as he started to stagger away from the swarm, the cloud of beetles thinned and then vanished.

None of the beetles had bitten him, or even latched on to his clothes. They had all brushed quickly by him and settled onto every open space in the workshop. The entire room was carpeted with beetles. Swarms of them had even landed on Sh'shak and Hoole. They were so startled that they nearly stopped their wingsong, but managed to keep it up as even more insects covered them.

Not only were the beetles no longer biting, but their angry drone had changed to a soft, gentle *whrrrr*. They were responding to the wingsong.

But for how long?

"We'd better hurry," Zak whispered to Tash.

It was weird, Zak thought, leaving Uncle Hoole buried under a pile of insects. But he tried to keep his mind on the job ahead. As carefully as they could, he and Tash stepped out of the workshop . . .

. . . and into a writhing sea of insects.

There were beetles everywhere. Millions of them, wriggling in circles on the ground, spreading out as far as the eye could see.

"Ugh," Tash said. "This is not going to be fun."

Walking on tiptoes, the two Arrandas made their way down the path, or at least what they thought was the path. The path had been buried under the insects.

Wherever they could, they stepped onto rocks or patches of bare ground. But more often, they simply had to step on the carpet of beetles, sinking up to their ankles in writhing bodies as they crushed dozens underfoot. Soon their shoes were soaked in goo that Zak didn't want to think about.

They hadn't gone far when they heard Thrawn storming up behind them. He made no comment as he waded quickly through the beetlefield toward his nearby shuttle.

"You know what he's going to do if he repairs his ship first," Tash whispered.

Zak nodded. "Call down his soldiers, and run a security check on us. We've got to move it."

They reached the halfway point between the workshop and their ship. They could see the garden arch just ahead, and beyond it lay the *Shroud*. Wingsong had drifted toward them all the time, keeping the beetles in a trance. But they could see that the effect of the wingsong was starting to wear off. The beetles had difficulty keeping still, and their herky-jerky movements made them bump into each other, causing a chain reaction.

Worse still, the farther Zak and Tash got from the workshop, the fainter the wingsong became. As they reached the garden arch, they could see small clouds of beetles rising into the air, then settling back down. The insects were growing restless.

The *whrrr* of the swarm began to deepen into a threatening hum.

"We're not going to make it," Tash whispered fearfully.

"Run!" Zak urged.

The two Arrandas broke into a sprint, smashing through the beetles that still surrounded them. They sprang though the arch. There were fewer beetles outside the wall, and their footing was better.

Tash and Zak reached the ship and climbed aboard just in time. Behind them, the beetles rose up from the ground in one giant layer, like a huge cloak being lifted over the garden. The wingsong was losing its power over them.

Inside the *Shroud*, Zak and Tash sealed the door and ran back to the engine room. "We're going to have the same problem we had on the Imperial shuttle," Zak reminded his sister. "If those bugs decide they want in, they'll come right through the vents."

Tash nodded. "I'll try to slow them down. You get to

work." She shook her head worriedly. "You know Zak, you wanted to fix your mistake all by yourself. Well, here's your chance. Don't let us down!"

Zak didn't bother to reply. He had already snapped off the maintenance panel, and found himself staring at the wiring he had damaged a few days before. Uncle Hoole had been able to replace the blown circuits, repair the damaged power couplings, and get the engines ready for re-ignition. Now all Zak had to do was repair the damage he had originally caused.

"Hurry, Zak!" Tash called.

He glanced back down the corridor. Tash was standing in the hall pressing a tray against the air vent. Zak thought he saw something small crawling across the ceiling over her head.

Zak tried to concentrate. He could do this. All he had to do was concentrate.

"Zak!" Tash urged. He heard her smash her palm against the wall, killing something.

Zak replaced several wires that had shorted out, and popped a power coil out of its small casing. Using a wire brush he cleaned it off, then replaced it.

"There!" he said.

But the ship was still dead.

"Hurry!" Tash pleaded.

He had no time to look back at her. He'd forgotten something. His eyes settled on the green-and-white cable. Of course! It was the same wire he'd moved the other day—it was still connected to the wrong socket! Zak plucked it out . . . then paused.

Where did it go again?

He'd forgotten where he'd moved it *from*.

"Aggghghhh!" Tash yelled.

"Now or never," he muttered. He closed his eyes and tried to remember what the maintenance panel looked like just before he'd messed with it. Then, opening his eyes, he chose one of the open sockets and jabbed the wire into the connection.

Lights went on all over the ship.

"Got it!" he yelled.

Zak bolted down the hall. Tash was still there, struggling to keep the vent blocked with one hand as she used the other to swipe a dozen drog beetles from her face and neck. Zak paused to pluck two beetles from her hair, then ran to the cockpit and dove over the pilot's chair to reach a tiny control knob.

"Vents closed!" he called out.

They were sealed in tight.

It took only a moment to help Tash kill the rest of the beetles. Then they activated the engines. A moment later, the *Shroud* was airborne.

Thunk! thunk! thunk!

The ship hurtled through a kilometer-long wall of insects, cutting a wide path through the dark cloud. They could see nothing through the viewscreen—the bodies of living and dead beetles covered the transparasteel window.

As Tash piloted the ship, Zak used the scanner to lock onto Hoole's readings, and they guided the ship toward the workshop.

"How are we going to get them out of there?" Zak asked.

Tash grinned. "Hey, you're already the hero. Leave the piloting to me."

Smoothly, Tash guided the *Shroud* to a gentle landing— only a few inches from the workshop door. Zak ran back and opened the hatch just as two figures stumbled out of the doorway. The figures plunged through clouds of beetles toward the entrance to the *Shroud*. Grabbing their out-stretched hands, Zak hauled them onboard.

As the ship rose into the air again, Zak was on his feet, slapping away the bugs that had clung stubbornly to Hoole and Sh'shak.

Like a warrior counting his trophies, Zak counted as he stomped the biting insects.

By the time Hoole and Sh'shak were cleaned off, he was grinning. He had killed exactly thirty.

EPILOGUE

Zak had just climbed out of the sonic shower onboard the *Shroud*. They'd flown a safe distance from the swarm and landed again on a bug-free part of the planet. Zak, Tash, and Uncle Hoole had each cleaned themselves at least three times, and still the feeling of something crawling across their skin would not go away.

"I used your ship's comlink to notify our leaders," Sh'shak was saying to Hoole. "A fleet of airships is on its way."

"Will they destroy the beetles?" Tash asked.

"I think not," the S'krrr replied. "The beetles will be caught, and the population spread around the planet. After all, as you saw, when the balance of nature is maintained, the beetles are most beneficial to vegetation. However, from now on we'll keep a closer watch on how the garden is maintained."

Hoole nodded. "And now we must be going. Thrawn may have already gotten his ship operational. It would not be wise for us to be here when his reinforcements arrive."

Sh'shak extended his clawlike insect hand to Tash and Hoole, then paused when he reached Zak. "It was extremely fortunate that you were here to help us. A few more months, perhaps even a few more days, and there would have been too many beetles to stop. They would have overrun the planet."

Zak blushed. "If I'd said something about that shreev earlier, you might have learned about Vroon's scheme."

"Perhaps," Sh'shak replied, "or perhaps you would simply have told Vroon and he would have convinced you there was no problem. In any case, the problem will soon be solved."

Zak nodded, thinking, *Yes, and that's the last time I try to fix something without asking for help!*

The *Shroud*'s hatch closed. "Let's go," Hoole said to his niece and nephew. "I've had enough insects for one day."

None of them noticed the two small figures scuttle across the ceiling. Two insects froze as the three humanoids stomped down the corridor. When Hoole and the Arrandas were gone, the beetles waggled their antennae, sensing warmth. Then they scurried along the ceiling toward the warm engine room.

A perfect place to lay their eggs . . .

Hoole, Tash, and Zak continue their journeys to the darkest reaches of the galaxy in *Spore,* the next book in the Star Wars: Galaxy of Fear series. For a sneak preview, turn the page!

AN EXCERPT FROM

BOOK 9

SPORE

It happened so fast, Tash thought she was seeing things.

One moment, Zak was standing next to her.

The next, he was up in the branches of a nearby tree. For the first few seconds, Tash's brain couldn't figure out how it had happened—she thought her brother had somehow jumped up into the tree, and all she could do was wonder why he was thrashing around up there.

Then Zak managed a strangled cry of ''Help!'' and she knew he was in trouble.

The vines of the tree were moving. Sharp, jagged leaves protruded from the vines like claws. Several of the vines had already wrapped themselves around Zak's waist, and more were now encircling his neck and throat. When he tried to pry the vines away, tree branches whipped against his arms. "Hel—!" Zak started to yell again before a vine covered his mouth.

"Zak!" Tash shouted. She ran toward the tree.

Which was just what the tree wanted. The moment she stepped within range, a vine stabbed out to loop around her ankle. But the Force was with her. She moved as the vine moved and jumped back just in time.

The tree pulled Zak in even farther, and he nearly disappeared beneath the vines. But Tash could still see his feet kicking, and the thrashing vines told her that her brother was putting up a good fight.

Again and again Tash tried to rush forward, but each time the tree was waiting for her. Tash picked up a rock and threw it at the tree. The stone bounced off the tree's hard trunk—nothing happened. But she had no other weapon to use. In frustration, Tash picked up a larger rock.

"That won't help," said a deep, calm voice.

Tash nearly dropped the rock on her foot.

Standing behind her, gazing with calm, friendly eyes, was Fandomar the Ithorian.

"Help!" Tash insisted. "It'll kill him."

Without answering, Fandomar stepped past Tash and walked right into the shade of the thrashing tree. Over the hissing sound of scraping leaves, Tash heard Fandomar talk to the tree in a soft, throaty whisper. She couldn't understand the words, but the voice was so soothing that Tash felt instantly calm.

Fandomar's voice had the same effect on the tree. Its moving limbs became still. A thick bunch of vines suddenly unrolled toward the ground, revealing Zak, who had been wrapped up as tightly as a mummy from Necropolis. His face was a deep shade of red and his eyes looked like they'd almost been squeezed out of his head.

Still frightened of the tree, Tash kept an eye on its branches as she ran to her brother's side. She caught him just as his knees gave out.

"Are you hurt?" she asked.

Zak shook his head. "I'm okay." Then, with a gasp, he added, "Breathing—it's a very good thing."

"He should recover shortly," Fandomar said.

Tash moved quickly out of the shade of the predatory tree. "Your planet looks so peaceful," she said to the Ithorian. "I can't believe you have such dangerous trees. You should cut them down."

Fandomar stiffened, and Tash realized she had offended the Ithorian, who said, "We obey the Law of Life. We do not kill living things."

"But that tree almost killed Zak," Tash said, a little more gently.

Patiently, Fandomar opened her delicate fingers in a gesture like a human shrug. "The vesuvague is not dangerous. At least not to Ithorians."

"Vesu—?" Tash tried to repeat.

"Veh-soo-vog," Fandomar repeated slowly, pronouncing the word for her.

Zak coughed. When he felt that he could talk normally, he said, "Thanks, Fandomar. If you hadn't come by, I would have been plant food."

"What did you say to the tree?" Tash asked Fandomar.

The Ithorian replied, "It's not what I said, but how I said it. Ithorians—especially the High Priests—are very connected to the Mother Forest. They know how to speak to the trees."

"Then you're a High Priest?" Tash asked.

Fandomar waved her fingers again. *It* is *a shrug,* Tash thought. *It's what she does when she doesn't want to say anything.*

Fandomar walked them back to their skimmer. To Tash's surprise, she had landed her own little ship under the same overhang. Had Fandomar seen them land? Or was she just trying to hide her ship, too?

"I know we're not supposed to be down here,"

Tash quickly told Fandomar. "I'm sorry. We—I mean, *I*—just wanted to see the forest. We didn't realize—"

"I understand," Fandomar interrupted. "No harm has been done."

Tash thanked the stars that Ithorians were so understanding. She'd met plenty of species who would have screamed at them for disobeying local customs. She decided to push her luck.

"Um, there's one more thing. Do you think— I mean, would you mind not telling our uncle about this? As long as no harm was done."

The Ithorian nodded. "I agree. As long as you promise not to tell anyone that you saw me down here."

So Fandomar *had* wanted to hide her ship. "You aren't a High Priest, are you?" Tash guessed. "You're not supposed to be down here, either."

Fandomar nodded. "That is correct. But I think it's in both our interests to keep this secret to ourselves."

"Secrets," Zak groaned. On a recent visit to the planet S'krrr, he'd kept a secret that nearly cost them all their lives. "I swore I'd never keep a secret like this again."

"To seal our agreement," Fandomar said, "let me show you something few offworlders have ever seen."

———

They were standing at the edge of an enormous grove of trees with shining black bark. They weren't vesuvague trees. This was like a forest within the forest—a wood so thick and deep that Tash could hardly see beyond the first few branches.

"This is the oldest grove of Bafforr trees on Ithor," Fandomar explained. "Bafforr trees are sentient."

"Sentient?" Zak repeated.

"That means they can think. They're intelligent," Tash explained.

Fandomar nodded. "The more trees there are, the more intelligent the forest becomes. It's as though one mind connects them all so that they can all work together."

"Work together," Tash repeated. "Like a team. That's what I want." Louder, she asked, "Can we *talk* to them?"

Fandomar shook her head. "High Priests can. They are very sensitive to the Bafforrs' thoughts. But without that sensitivity, you cannot hear them."

Tash said, "It sounds like you're talking about the Force."

Fandomar's two mouths turned down. "No, the High Priests aren't Jedi Knights. Their sensitivity is different."

Tash wondered if she could reach the trees anyway. She'd only learned a little bit about the Force, but according to what she had read, the Force connected all living things. If that was true, why couldn't it connect her to the Bafforr trees?

Focusing her thoughts, she reached out with the Force. She took a deep breath to clear her head and then felt it—like an invisible hand stretching toward the forest. For just a brief instant, Tash felt something reach back in response. An excited tingle ran through her arms. The Bafforr trees were aware of her!

For that moment, she felt a powerful connection with the trees. Tash couldn't have described it if she'd tried. It was like . . . It was like playing speed globe with a really good team, with everyone working together. Only it was a thousand times more satisfying than just playing a game.

Excited, Tash pushed harder. She wanted to be a Jedi Knight. She *needed* to be one, but she had no way of testing herself. If she could communicate with the Bafforr trees, that might mean the Force was still with her, that her power was growing.

But she tried too hard. The more she thought about trying to use the Force, the harder it became to use it, until finally, it just slipped away.

"What's wrong, Tash?" Zak asked.

She sighed. Zak wouldn't understand. "Nothing. Come on, let's go."

She turned away from the forest, feeling lonelier than ever.

Fandomar followed them back to the *Tafanda Bay* and walked them to their quarters. Uncle Hoole had returned from his errands.

He studied his niece and nephew for a moment, as though he were bracing himself for bad news. When none came, his gray face twisted into a look of amusement. "This is a pleasure," he said. "I have left you alone for several hours, and nothing eventful has happened. No Imperial invasions. No dangerous criminals."

"We haven't uncovered one evil plot," Tash agreed, casually tossing her speed globe from hand to hand. "Did you get everything we need?"

Hoole frowned. "Unfortunately not. The Ithorians do not do much mining. I need a supply of the mineral ethromite."

"What's ethromite?" Tash asked.

Zak answered, "It's one of the minerals used to create the fusion reactions that power starship engines."

"And it seems to be in scarce supply here," Hoole added.

Fandomar raised one long finger to get their attention. "I believe I can help."

Not only did Fandomar know where they could acquire more ethromite, she offered to take Hoole and the two Arrandas there. Not far from the planet Ithor was a large asteroid field where a group of humans had set up a mining colony. Fandomar's job aboard the *Tafanda Bay* was to pilot a shuttle that ferried supplies to and from the mining colony. Although she was not scheduled to return to the colony for several days, she would be happy to take Hoole and the Arrandas out on a special mission.

A short time later, they climbed aboard an old but well-kept cargo ship and streaked out of the planet's atmosphere. Through the viewport Tash watched the stars rush toward the ship.

A short journey took them into a wide band of rocks whirling through space—asteroids. Some of the asteroids were as small as Tash's head, others seemed as big as moons. Some of the asteroids drifted by slowly, while others flashed by as fast as comets. Tash had still been holding the speed globe, but now she dropped it and gripped the edge of her seat until her knuckles turned white. One wrong turn in an asteroid field would turn them into an exploding fireball.

"This is dangerous work," Hoole stated.

Fandomar nodded, concentrating on the deadly rocks spinning past the ship. Tash closed her eyes.

"It seems like you get stuck with all the jobs no

one else wants," Zak noted. "Greeting people at the space dock, piloting shuttles. Don't you want to be doing something more important?"

Hoole winced at Zak's impoliteness, but Fandomar only nodded. "I am . . . doing penance."

"Penance?" Tash asked, opening one eye. "You mean you're being punished?"

"In a sense," the Ithorian explained. "Only . . . I have *chosen* these tasks. I have volunteered to make this run."

"Why?" Hoole asked. "I thought that Ithorians preferred not to travel too far from the Mother Forest and their herd ships."

"True," Fandomar replied. "But my husband was exiled from Ithor several years ago. Although he would not let me go with him, I swore to myself that I would not sit comfortably aboard the *Tafanda Bay* until his return."

"What did he do?" Zak asked.

Fandomar opened her twin mouths to reply. But instead, she suddenly jerked the controls hard to one side, throwing the ship into a confused spin.

For a moment Tash thought the Ithorian had gone crazy.

Until she saw the sharp teeth of the giant worm that was lunging to swallow their ship!

———

"Space slug!" Hoole warned.

Tash's eyes went wide with fear. She had never seen a space slug before. The slug had sprung from a cave in a nearby asteroid. The hole in the flying rock was large enough to let a starship through, and the slug filled every meter. Tash caught a glimpse of the thick gray body slithering out of its cave, and its huge eyeless head. But then the slug's body, the asteroids, even the stars around them, vanished as the space slug opened its huge jaws to swallow them.

Fandomar jerked on the controls again and the cargo ship lurched in the other direction. Tash's crash webbing snapped and she went flying, slamming her shoulder against the side of the ship.

Fandomar's move saved their lives. Instead of chomping on them, the space slug only tapped their ship with the side of its massive head. Their shields held, but the ship spun wildly out of control.

"We've got to get out of here," Hoole grunted. "Out of its range."

"No good," Fandomar replied. "The engines aren't responding."

Tash pointed to the asteroids rocketing through space around them. "We're drifting! One of those asteroids will hit us!"

"Not if the space slug gets us first!" Zak yelled.

They were still in the huge slug's range. Its head

and part of its body twisted wildly from the cave, trying to reach them. The slug turned its head toward them and opened its mouth to strike.

"Move the ship!" Tash yelled.

"I cannot!" Fandomar shouted back.

The space slug stabbed at them again.

But before it could reach them, the slug recoiled in pain as a streak of light punctured its skin.

Laser beams!

Someone was firing blaster bolts at the space slug.

The slug hesitated. It seemed to be attracted by the rapid movements and flashing lights of three tiny yellow ships that crisscrossed and zigzagged around the worm. The ships were hardly bigger than a human and they moved with incredible speed, flying circles around the giant slug. Laser beams flashed from the ships and penetrated the slug's skin like needles. As the three ships continued to pour fire onto the slug, the creature shut its mouth and coiled back into its hole.

"Cargo ship, this is Starfly One," said a welcoming voice over Fandomar's comm. "Looks like you could use a little help."

The three small craft formed a triangle around Fandomar's damaged cargo cruiser and locked onto it with tractor beams. One Starfly pulled them, while the others pushed the cargo ship forward with their beams. Once they had the larger ship under control, they headed back toward the asteroid field.

"We're not going back there, are we?" Tash gasped, as a huge asteroid flew by.

"Have no fear," Fandomar explained calmly. "The Starflies are specifically designed for flight through the asteroids. They're small and maneuverable enough to get around the rocks. Their tractor beams can push as well as pull. The miners use them to move space rocks out of their paths, but they'll work just as well at moving us. These miners know how to handle asteroids."

She was right. The pilots seemed to have a sixth sense for where the space rocks would move. Even hauling the damaged cargo ship, they slipped easily through the gaps in the swarm of asteroids.

In a few moments, the Starflies dropped toward an asteroid that was almost the size of a planet. Tash saw a small collection of buildings clinging to its rocky surface. The Starflies hauled their passengers into a small docking bay. Tash, Zak, and Hoole waited until the docking-bay door had closed and oxygen had flooded into the chamber.

They hopped out of their ship and hurried to the nearest Starfly.

"Look how small these ships are!" Zak said appreciatively. "They're hardly bigger than a landspeeder. I can't believe they have enough room for life-support systems."

"They do not," Fandomar answered. "The pilots must wear space suits while flying."

Just then the Starfly's hatch broke open and a large human in a flight suit and helmet jumped out. He gave a few orders to his two companions, who hurried from the docking bay. As the big man removed his helmet, Tash saw short-cropped gray hair and a friendly smile. The man shook their hands and said, "Welcome to Mining Station Alpha. I'm the chief miner, but we're a small outfit here, just me and the other two, so just call me Hodge."

Hoole bowed slightly. "We owe you our thanks. That slug would have swallowed us in moments."

Hodge nodded. "The asteroid field's infested with them. I knew one of those giant worms would get Fandomar one of these days."

"I was distracted," the Ithorian admitted, coming up behind.

"So!" Hodge clapped his hands together eagerly. "We don't get many visitors out here. What can we do for you?"

Hoole told Hodge the same story he'd told Fandomar, giving few details. "We need ethromite to power our ship."

Hodge nodded. "We got plenty of that. It may cost you, though."

Hoole nodded. "I am sure I have enough credits—"

Hodge waved his hands and grinned. "Nope, don't need credits. We make plenty off the Ithorians here." He chuckled at Fandomar. "I'd rather make a trade. If you're an anthropologist, you may be able to answer a few questions. I'll give you all the ethromite you need, if you help us solve a little mystery."

Tash watched Hoole's expression. She could tell he wanted to get the ethromite as quickly as possible, but she also knew that he loved to explore different cultures. "Very well. As long as it will put the children in no danger."

"Naw!" the big miner laughed. "No danger. Just a little space walk is all."

An hour later, Tash found herself walking on the surface of the asteroid. She was wearing a bulky space suit and a clear round fishbowl of a helmet. On her back she carried an oxygen tank and a small computer—the brains of the suit. The computer maintained a constant temperature inside the suit and pumped oxygen into her helmet.

Tash's heart pounded against her ribs. She craned

her neck forward and touched her nose to the plastiform faceplate of her helmet. Only a thin sheet of plastiform protected her from the icy cold vacuum of space. Only a few layers of protective fabric kept her from instant death.

"Look up, Tash," Zak said. She heard his voice through the comlink speaker in her helmet.

Tash looked up and immediately felt dizzy. The asteroid field was just as frightening as before. In fact, it was scarier. Rocks the size of mountains hurtled over their heads. She felt just like one of the space rocks herself—spinning around, hurtling alone through the dark vacuum.

"There's no 'up' in space, laser brain," she told Zak irritably. "And there's no down, either. That's because there isn't any gravity."

Tash stamped her feet slowly. Her thick boots kicked up a cloud of dust that hung over the ground. The boots were specially designed for use on asteroids with zero gravity. Normal gravity boots—the kind used in space ships—were equipped with magnetic soles so that they would stick to the metal of the ship. But since the ground on an asteroid was nonmagnetic, the miners used boots equipped with mini-tractor beams instead of magnets. The tractor beams pulled her feet toward the ground. On the planet Ithor, she would hardly be able to lift these boots. But in the weightlessness of space, they all had to wear special grav-boots to keep from floating right off the asteroid.

They were marching along the asteroid's surface, with Hodge in the lead. Fandomar followed Hodge in a space suit specially designed to fit Ithorians' bodies. Then came Zak and Tash. Hoole brought up the rear.

Hodge led them to the edge of a giant pit. Unlike the rough surface of the asteroid, the sides of the pit were very smooth, as if something had been sliding in and out of it for years.

"A slug hole," Tash guessed.

"Right," Hodge's voice crackled over the comlink. "But the slug's long gone."

"How do we get down there?" Zak asked, peering down into the rocky tunnel.

"Like this," the miner said.

He jumped into the hole.

Without gravity, he might have hung in empty space forever. But his grav-boots pulled him downward, and slowly he began to descend into the slug tunnel. Fandomar followed a moment later.

Zak and Tash looked at Hoole, who gave the slightest nod.

They all jumped.

Tash fell in super slow motion. She had plenty of time for her eyes to adjust to the dark tunnel, and she watched the bottom slowly rise up to meet her. The tunnel wasn't very deep. It dropped straight down for a few dozen meters, then curved sharply to one side and leveled off. She landed at the curve with an easy bounce.

Hodge had lit a bright glowrod and motioned for them to follow him.

The cavern was huge. The slug that filled the hole must have been a hundred meters thick.

Tash slid her hand along the wall as they continued their hike. It was as smooth as glass. She could hardly believe that any creature lived in deep space. It was amazing that the slugs didn't need air to breathe or sunlight for warmth.

Deep in thought, Tash didn't notice that the walls were closing in. The tunnel was tapering off. She didn't notice that the others had stopped moving until she bumped into something hard and gray standing in front of her. She looked up . . .

. . . into the face of an Ithorian, standing there without a space suit, its two mouths twisted into a look of absolute terror!

Tash let out a warning shout right into her comlink microphone. Everyone around her jumped as the sound of her voice blasted into their helmets.

Zak put his gloved hands on the sides of his helmet

like he was trying to plug his ears. "Tash! Turn down the volume. It's only a—"

A statue. She could see that now. It was a statue of an Ithorian. It was holding both hands up in a warning gesture. In the light of Hodge's glowrod, the statue's face looked both angry and frightened.

"Curious," Hoole muttered. He was talking to himself, but they could all hear him as clearly as they'd heard Tash shout. The Shi'ido stepped past the statue. The tunnel ended just a few meters beyond. Set into the very end of the tunnel was a thick durasteel door.

Hodge pointed up to a hole in the tunnel ceiling. A shaft had been dug down from the surface of the asteroid. The chief miner explained, "We were digging down from the surface, looking for minerals. Our laser drill broke through into this empty space. We knew it had to be a worm tunnel, so we found the tunnel opening and used it to get down here. We found this."

"Fandomar," Hoole said after he'd examined the statue for a moment. "I was not aware that the Ithorians made statues like this. Most Ithorian artwork involves plants and animals. What do you make of this?"

Fandomar raised her hands. "I couldn't say."

Hodge held his glowrod up to the statue's face. "I've been around Ithorians enough to know their expressions. This one looks angry or frightened. Or both."

"It's like a warning," Tash said.

Zak scoffed. "There are a lot better ways to warn people," he said. "How about a holographic message? Warning beacons. Signs."

Hodge answered. "All that kind of stuff was here. At least we think it was."

He pointed to a section of the tunnel wall near the statue. Someone had cut an alcove into the smooth rock. In the alcove they saw the remains of a generator and a few strands of cable. The cable wires had been cut.

"This is how we found it," the chief miner explained. "Me and my boys don't normally go into worm holes. But we got readings on a good supply of minerals down here, so we risked it and found this. That doorway is sealed shut. We didn't know what to make of it."

"Maybe you should report it to the Ithorians," Tash suggested.

"We did," Hodge said, nodding toward Fandomar.

Fandomar blinked. "My people had no response."

Hoole looked from the statue to the cut wires and back to the statue again. Finally, he said, "I believe the statue *is* a warning. I suspect it is some sort of fail-safe in case the power supply for the true warning device ever failed." Hoole pointed to the base of the statue. A long rectangular section of the stone looked discolored. "It looks like someone removed something from the statue. Probably there was a written warning carved into the stone."

Tash bent down to examine the spot. There had been a sign there. She could see that part of it had broken when the mysterious intruders had snapped it off. Even if Tash could have read the language, only parts of the words were visible.

"So who removed the warning?" Zak asked.

"And who put it here in the first place?" Tash added.

"Ithorians, obviously," Hoole decided. "I would guess that what lays behind that door is a tomb. But the question is: Why would Ithorians, who rarely leave their home planet, fly out to this barren asteroid field to bury someone, or something, in the bottom of a worm tunnel?"

Hodge grunted. "I was hoping you could help, being an anthropologist and all. I guess there's only one way to find out what it is."

Hoole shook his head. "I think we should get the permission of the Ithorians before doing anything here."

The chief miner replied, "It's not really their call. Me and my men own this rock now. I've been itching to find out what's behind this door. Whether it's a tomb or not, I figure there must be something important down here for someone to go to so much trouble. Could be worth a lot of money. If you can't tell me, I know another way to find out."

He strode past the statue toward the sealed door behind it. Tash noticed he had brought a long metal bar with him. It looked like a cross between an ax and a pry bar. With an expert thrust he jammed it into the door frame.

"No!" Fandomar suddenly shouted. "Stop!"

Hodge ignored her and pried at the door. The seal looked very old, but it held firm. He leaned his weight into his next push. A tiny crack appeared in the seal.

At that moment, Tash heard a tremendous *BOOM!* from behind them, and the solid rock beneath their feet shook as though a groundquake had begun. A cloud of dust shot up and hung in the air like a curtain.

When the dust cleared, they could see that an enormous block of stone had dropped from the ceiling of the tunnel and crashed to the floor, closing off the way they had entered.

They were trapped inside the asteroid.

ABOUT THE AUTHOR

John Whitman has written several interactive adventures for *Where in the World Is Carmen Sandiego?*, as well as many Star Wars stories for audio and print. He is an executive editor for Time Warner AudioBooks and lives in Encino, California.

Journey to a galaxy far, far away with these other

exciting ⟍⟍TAR WAR⟋ books

Shadows of the Empire
A Junior Novelization by Christopher Golden, Based
on the *New York Times* Bestseller

And read more about the Star Wars heroes
in new stories that take up where
Return of the Jedi left off:

#1 *The Glove of Darth Vader*
#2 *The Lost City of the Jedi*
#3 *Zorba the Hutt's Revenge*
#4 *Mission from Mount Yoda*
#5 *Queen of the Empire*
#6 *Prophets of the Dark Side*

Is the force with you?

To find out read...

CHOOSE YOUR OWN
STAR WARS®
ADVENTURE™

A NEW HOPE

Limited Collector Edition 3-D Hologram Cover!

CHRISTOPHER GOLDEN

LIMITED COLLECTOR'S EDITION

0-553-48651-9

Available March 9, 1998, wherever books are sold.

Join Luke, Princess Leia, and Han Solo and fight against the evil Galactic Empire—only this time *you* control the twists, turns, and outcomes of the most exciting adventure in the galaxy. Will you lead the Rebellion to victory against the Empire? Or side with Darth Vader and betray your friends? The fate of the galaxy is in *your* hands in this interactive novel based on the original *Star Wars* film.

BFY